Dirty Laundry

A LAUNDROMAT AND DOG WASH ROMANCE

SMALL TOWN DIRT
BOOK THREE

REGINA BERGEN

For Eriko (@ErikoReads),
whose "select-a-scene" support helped fund this book and whose love of stories shines brighter than any laundromat fluorescent light.
The first Yappy Hour scene exists because of you.
Thank you for believing in this story—and for building such a beautiful space for books and readers alike on your social media.
Readers: Go follow her. You'll be glad you did.

For Melanie,
who signed up to support this book through 'create-a-pet'... and somehow unleashed the star of the show.
Sir Walter the Bouvier—inspired by your own dog (follow him on Instagram!)—stole every scene he bear-walked into, just like you do at my events dressed as a sunflower, a coffee cup, or whatever wild costume comes next.
You've been my cheerleader, my unpaid assistant, my walking billboard, and my friend since we were kids.
Every author needs a Melanie. I'm lucky you're mine.

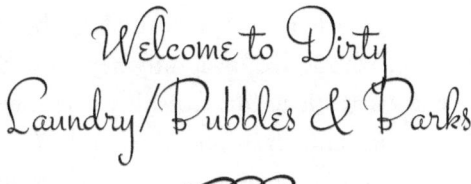

Welcome to Dirty Laundry/Bubbles & Parks

CLAIRE

Chapter 1

"WALTER—NO! WALTER—GET OUT OF THERE! SIR Walter the Bouvier, you get out of there right this instant!" Claire scowled, stomping her feet like an angry toddler as she pulled her dog's collar firmly but gently, trying, without success, to pull him out from *inside* a pile of warm, clean laundry. In mere moments, he had transformed the lavender-scented pile into a makeshift bed, complete with blankets to burrow under. She only used his full name when she was angry with him—and she *was*!

"I just finished drying those clothes, Walt!" Claire

1

rolled her eyes as she released her grip on his collar. The laundry was already covered in dog hair... it was pretty much a lost cause at that point. "I walk away for *two minutes* to greet the delivery man, and this is what I get," she mumbled under her breath. "At least they were *my* clothes this time," she added, resigning herself to the fate of re-washing the entire load or finishing the week off by making a dog-hair chic fashion statement. *I mean, I'm usually covered in dog hair anyway... I don't really think it would surprise anyone.*

Claire glanced down at Walter and sighed. A moment later, the bell on the front door of *Dirty Laundry/Bubbles & Barks* clanged as the door swung open. Walt's ears perked at the sound. Then, without a moment's hesitation, he rose from his clothing camouflage and trotted over to the half-door separating the main area of the laundromat from the office. He jumped up, placing two giant paws on top of the half-door so he could peer out, covering the surface with drool. He barked once and appeared to be considering a more lengthy, loud vocalization when Claire placed a hand on his head.

"Don't even think about it," she said. "Down." She gently urged Walt off the half-door, then squeezed past her dog, holding him back to prevent him from following her out. "No way, dude. I don't think so," she said, glancing down as he tried to slip past her. "You, stay."

"Good morning, Mr. Manuelo. Whatcha got for me today?" Claire called out, smiling at the older gentleman who had walked in during Walt's antics.

"Ahh, hello, Claire. What's that I heard back there? Is Mr. Walter giving you a hard time again?"

"Sir Walter," she gently reminded her long-time customer. "And yes, he certainly is. When isn't he? Sometimes I wonder whether having a shop dog was the best decision... especially Walt."

"Don't be silly. You would miss him if he wasn't here every day. All of us would, and don't you forget it. Since *Bubbles & Barks* was added, it is a lot more fun to do laundry—or even to drop it off, in my case! You've certainly shaken things up since your parents' time."

"Well, I'm not sure how my parents would feel about some of my decisions around here, but... you're right about one thing: I wouldn't know what to do here without him. It keeps things interesting, and the other dogs coming in and out make us both happy! I just wish Walt wasn't such a troublemaker."

"Ahh, he's still young yet. Give him time. He'll grow out of it!"

"Mr. Manuelo... he's almost five. He's hardly a puppy anymore."

"Has it been that long already? I remember when he was just a tiny little thing." As if on command, Walt poked his head over the half-door, rested his paws on the ledge, and let out a whine. Mr. Manuelo walked over to greet him. "Then again, I remember when *you* were just a girl playing on the laundry carts, using them as racecars. Now, look at you both!"

Mr. Manuelo turned his attention to Walt. "Sorry, bud. I didn't mean to ignore you." He petted Walter behind his ears. "The usual, Claire—wash, dry, and fold, please. No rush. I'll be on a business trip for the next few days, so I'll be back on Thursday or Friday to pick up."

"Perfect. I'll have it ready for you by Thursday. Come in whenever you want."

"Thank you, as always, young lady. And, as for you, Walter, my friend, I must get moving. I haven't even started packing, and I'm supposed to be on a flight to D.C. this afternoon." He gave the dog a final scratch under his chin and turned toward the exit. "And, remember, take it easy on Claire, Walt. She's one of the good ones."

"So are you, Mr. Manuelo. Walter is a great judge of character—and he's always liked you so much. Have a safe trip!" With that, the man offered a smile and a quick wave over his shoulder, then left the laundromat.

"Alright, Walt. Mr. Manuelo's been in. What's next on the agenda besides re-washing the clothes you decided to use as a nap mat?" Claire chuckled as she walked back into the office, plopping down on the chair in front of her desk. She glanced at a list resting on her work area, scanned the items, and muttered something under her breath when she reached the one she'd highlighted in green. Green meant money. Green had been a big problem lately.

"Ahh, machine 3. The largest capacity dryer. Broken. Again. Time for me to don my maintenance hat, I guess. Certainly can't afford the repairman this week. It'd sure be easier if I had some more handy help around here."

As Claire finished her sentence, almost as if he understood, Walter let out a slight bark. "Oh, I know. I know. You're *tons* of help, Walt." She grinned. "I didn't mean to offend you." Claire reached down and patted her dog's head, causing him to drop to the floor like a sack of potatoes (with seemingly no concern about the toll it'd take on his body!), and roll onto his back for belly rubs.

Claire smiled. She loved his floor flop. She crouched and rubbed the dog's stomach, hitting the ticklish spot that made him kick his legs in the air repeatedly, causing her to laugh out loud.

"Alright, play time's over, boy. It's time to get back to work!" Claire said, rising to her feet and grabbing a wrench and a screwdriver from the counter beside her desk. As she approached the half-door, the bell on the entrance rang again. She glanced at the door and brightened.

"Claire! Long time no see, girl. How's the laundry and dog wash business treating ya?"

"Carla, hey! How's it going? What're you doing here? You're *never* here. You have your own washer and dryer. Oh! Oh! Did you get a dog?!"

"Oh, God, no. You know better than anyone that Matt and I can barely take care of ourselves. The last thing we need is another living, breathing entity to attempt to keep alive. I killed Gia's lavender when she trusted her plants with me to go on a site visit to some eco-tourism destination with Ben in like... I don't know, Tahiti or something. It's comforter day, though. Matt says they're gross, and I got sick of listening to him whine—so here I am! It's so much faster here."

Claire laughed. "Good point," she admitted, remembering the time all of her high school classmates had been given fake babies to care for to earn extra credit in Home Economics. Carla's "baby" somehow returned to school with a kitchen knife sticking out from its head and a designer scarf as a diaper. Carla and Gia were Claire's oldest friends. Each of their significant others attended the same school as well. What could she say? Small-town life and love.

Honestly, the way Gia and Ben wound up together was a story in itself, one worthy of its own novel! Claire could only hope to experience such a romance, but in the meantime, she was happy to get updates from Carla, a known gossip whose heart was in the right place, about her friends' lives when they didn't have time to meet up in person. They'd all been so busy lately!

"How are Gia and Ben doing—and you and Matt?"

"Oh, Matt and I are just... well... Matt and I. We're good! He's a pain in my ass, as always." Carla grinned at Claire. "You know how it is with us. Gia and Ben are great! *Cold Brew* and *Charmed to Table* are really doing well. Gia has revamped the restaurant into something truly magical. It's like experiencing edible art every time, and the place is such a vibe. We should go together sometime!"

"You know I'd love to, but I am stuck here almost all the time. It's been hard since my parents passed away. I can't afford to close early, and I don't have the budget to hire any staff members. It's hard to find time for myself."

Carla rested her hand on her friend's shoulder. "I know, girl. I know. Hopefully, things will get easier soon. Where's Walt? He's being so quiet..."

Suddenly, a look of unadulterated terror crossed Claire's face. "Oh shit. You're right. He is. Even when the bell rang. That's... that's *never* good!" She took off running toward the office, followed closely behind by Carla, and pressed her hands against the half-door, peering inside. Her jaw dropped.

"Oh—my—God!" Carla's words interrupted Claire's stunned silence.

The words prompted Claire's own voice to return. "SIR WALTER THE BOUVIER! What have you done?!" Claire shouted, burying her face in her hands.

There, in the center of the office, was Walt, trying unsuccessfully to remain on his feet while attempting to escape from a giant, slippery pool of blue laundry detergent. It was still oozing from the industrial-sized bottle he had knocked from a low shelf, cracking it and causing it to spread quickly. By the time Claire and Carla noticed, the detergent coated most of the floor's surface area, creating something akin to a blue ice-skating rink. The aroma could only be described as... overpoweringly, overwhelmingly *fresh*.

Seeing his owner, Walt attempted to make a run for it in Claire's direction, but his legs flew out from under him. He fell to the floor in a heap, gazing up at Carla and Claire sheepishly. Claire groaned as she began removing her shoes and socks, preparing to enter the room and come to his aid.

"I'll just... I'll just go get my comforters started," Carla declared, wincing at the scene before her and excusing herself from the disaster to handle her own task. It reminded Claire of the time they went to that high school party together, and when the police showed up, she—Claire's ride home—was nowhere to be found! Carla wasn't a bad friend; she just suffered from shortsighted decisions and a powerful, sometimes misguided, sense of self-preservation.

Walt remained frozen in place, his legs sprawled to the sides. He was too afraid to move and risk falling again. As Claire slid through the room in bare feet, she used the walls, then her desk, gripping them to provide at least some balance as she maneuvered over the slippery floor. She grabbed a mop that was leaning against the wall as she passed, moving toward her desk. As she glanced at it, her eyes caught a line on the 'to-do' list. She couldn't help but laugh as she grabbed a pen, crossed off 'mop office floor,' and continued toward Walt, using the dry mop to push the detergent aside as best she could to create a *slightly* less treacherous path.

"Don't worry, buddy. I'm coming, Walt." She just hoped he hadn't been hurt in the fall or consumed any detergent.

The Veterinarian

~~~

CLAIRE

Chapter 2

BY THE TIME CLAIRE WAS HALFWAY BETWEEN THE desk and Walt, he was, once again, trying without success to stand to get to her. "No. Stay. Sit, stay," she ordered, forgetting in the chaos of the moment that Walter *only* responded to commands if his name was used directly before them. As soon as she realized her error, she had already reached him —but for good measure, she tried again.

"Walter, you quirky son-of-a-bitch... literally... SIT!" He sat, then looked up at her for further instructions. Claire rolled her eyes. *Of course.* "Walter, stay." He remained still as she wiped as much of the detergent as she could from the bottoms of his paws with her shirt. Walking behind him, she used both hands to push him from his rear, effectively sliding the dog across the floor on his bottom to the area the detergent hadn't reached.

She shook her head. Walter was an oddball. Always had been. All signs pointed to the likelihood that he probably always would be. Once they were clear of the slickest parts of the floor, Claire rose to her own feet and grabbed a damp cloth to remove the remaining detergent from his feet.

"Paw," she told her dog. Nothing. "Walter... paw," she tried again, muttering under her breath as she commanded him by name. Immediately, Walt raised his paw, making it easier for her to wipe it off, and then they repeated the process on the other side.

"You're going to need a full bath, but until we make sure you're okay, this will have to do."

"Is he okay?" came Carla's voice from the doorway, sensing the height of the chaos had subsided.

"I think so. I'm going to take him to the vet, just in case. I'll have to close early—but you're welcome to stick around and finish up your laundry without me."

"Don't be silly. Don't close. I'll handle things around here. How hard could it be? Surprisingly, I *do* know how to wash, dry, and fold, and I have to wash my comforters anyway," Carla said, shrugging. "I'll just leave anything weird for when you get back!"

"Are you sure? I don't want to mess up your day if this takes longer than expected."

"That's what old friends are for, isn't it? Take our friend Walt to the vet, and I'll hold down the fort until you get back."

"Carla, you're the best! Thank you so much. I'll call you as soon as I know something."

"Sure, sure. Take your time. We need to make sure Walt is okay. But, uh... just one thing..." Carla's voice trailed off.

"What's that?" Claire asked, her eyebrow raised.

"This," Carla said, gesturing at the office full of detergent and—now—suds from the chaos of moving Walter, "is a you problem. A problem for future Claire."

Claire grinned. "Deal. Thank you again," Claire said, clipping Walter to a leash and watching as he walked to get a sense of whether anything was injured. "He seems okay, but... I just want to be sure."

"Claire?"

"Yeah?"

"Stop talking and go. Now." Carla waved Claire toward the door dismissively.

"Okay. Going. Thank you again."

"Say hello to Dennis for me!" Carla shouted after Claire as she walked out the front door of the combination laundromat and dog wash.

Fortunately, the vet's office was nearby. Claire called on the way to let the receptionist know the circumstances and when they would arrive. As small-town life would have it, the vet was also a schoolmate of Claire's, but he was several years older. They'd gotten to know one another better through Walt's medical care. Walt had required a significant amount of medical care over the years!

It was only a ten-minute drive, and they arrived without further incident. Claire pulled into a parking spot in the lot beside the building, a small, home-looking structure consisting of a dance studio on one side and the veterinarian's office on the other. As Claire released Walt from the back passenger door, clipping his leash onto his collar, she examined the way he moved from the vehicle. *He seems okay. Moving normally, I think. Crazy as always.*

She chuckled, realizing that the way Walter moved was actually far from 'normal' to begin with. From behind, his breed—the bouvier—looked almost like a lumbering bear walking. Their relatively large size and black coloring further boosted the image.

By the time they entered the vet's office, after several stops to bark at ballet-dancing toddlers through the front window and more than a few attempts to chase a squirrel gathering nuts, Claire was fairly confident that Walt was just fine. Regardless, they went to see the vet to confirm—they were already there, after all.

As they entered the veterinarian's office, Walt's ears perked up at the sound of a booming, male voice. "Claire and Sir Walter, good to see you both. I hear you had a run-in with some soap, Walt." Dr. Dennis Porter crouched down to eye-level with Walter, a movement requiring significantly less downward motion than it would for many dog breeds. Everyone called him Dr. Dennis—and Claire had already been asked more than a few times to call him, simply, Dennis.

"Hi, Dr. Dennis," Claire began.

"Dennis. Just Dennis," he insisted.

"Dennis," she smiled. "Walt is... Walt is.... Well, Walt is an idiot, basically." She chuckled as she glanced at her dog, who seemed no worse for the wear given the events that had transpired back at the laundromat. "But we both already

11

knew that! Where's Rose?" Claire asked, glancing at the vacant receptionist desk.

The vet let out a rumbling chuckle. "Rose had to leave early today. Sick kid at home. So, I'm wearing multiple hats for the rest of the afternoon. An idiot, huh? Is that your official pet-owner diagnosis? It sounds about right, given Walter's track record," he said, thumbing through the file in his hand. "Ate a whole lobster, several sticks of butter, mouth burns after chewing on a laptop cord... It's really a miracle this dog is as healthy as he appears to be, really. It's kind of a miracle he's even *alive.*"

"I know. Trust me, I know. He has been... uh... challenging."

"Well, at least we get to spend a significant amount of time together." Dr. Dennis laughed softly.

Claire smiled. *I can never tell if he is flirting with me or if it's all in my head. Maybe he's like this with everyone... He's been divorced for a few years now...* Claire snapped herself back to the topic at hand.

"Do you think he will be okay? He may have licked *some* of the detergent, but I don't think he ingested very much. Once he realizes something doesn't taste good, he usually stops. And he seems to be walking alright... but I'm pretty sure he fell a few times. I was worried about his hips."

"Honestly, I think he'll be perfectly fine. I'll do an exam to check for injuries or areas of pain, and you'll need to monitor him for the next 24 hours—but he probably didn't consume much, as you said. Plus, he's *clearly* got a strong constitution," Dr. Dennis rested a hand on Claire's shoulder, "as indicated by the full recoveries from his past transgressions and misadventures."

The vet walked Claire and Walt to the first exam room, then, upon entering, kneeled to meet him at dog-level.

"Alright, Sir Walter the Bouvier, let's check you out," he said, putting a dog treat out on his hand for Walt, who quickly devoured it then licked Dr. Dennis's face. Dr. Dennis grinned. "Good boy." From this position, the vet carefully massaged around the dog's joints, checking for possible points of pain or swelling. Satisfied that Walt was relatively pain-free, Dr. Dennis rose.

"So far, so good," he confirmed, and Claire breathed a sigh of relief.

"He may be a little sore tomorrow, but nothing seems broken. One last thing..." Dr. Dennis walked from one side of the small exam room to the other, calling Walt over to each corner, then offering a treat as a reward. As the dog moved quickly from one side to the other seeking treats, the vet carefully took in his motions. "Sir Walt has nothing to worry about, and neither do you. He's as good as new," he concluded.

"Thank goodness," Claire exclaimed, grinning. "He really is a challenge, but I don't know what I'd do without him." She called her dog over and scratched behind his ears.

"He's a good dog. Well, maybe not *good*, per se, but sweet. Great temperament. Be sure to keep an eye on him for the next 24 hours. Just in case he got into more of the detergent than you thought. I'll give you my cell number so you can reach me in an emergency..." His voice trailed off as he jotted several numbers onto a post-it and handed it to Claire.

"Thank you so much, Dr. De—"

"Just Dennis."

"Thank you, Dennis."

"Always happy to see you two—although preferably not under these circumstances. Hey, Claire, uh... that cell number can be used for reasons other than a pet-related emergency, too. Like if you ever want to talk or text... or even go out for coffee or a walk, or maybe dinner."

Dennis seemed nervous. His final sentence came out in a tumble of words, and it took Claire a moment to process his intent. *Oh. I guess he **was** flirting.*

"Oh, okay... uh, thanks," she mumbled awkwardly, uncertain how to formulate an appropriate response. Her mind was in a hundred different places, none of which was forming a romantic attachment to her veterinarian. It's not that he wasn't cute—he was. He absolutely was, but Claire didn't feel any spark when he was near. To her, he gave off older brother vibes, and she refused to settle for less than pure magic this time around.

Maybe I'll text him. Maybe I won't. Maybe he just needs to grow on me. I just never really thought of him in that way before. Lost in thought, Claire gave a noncommittal shrug, then grabbed Walt's leash and awkwardly smiled and waved to Dr. Dennis before bolting to the door and escaping to her car.

The Coffee Catastrophe

CLAIRE

Chapter 3

Upon returning to the laundromat, Claire pulled open the door tentatively, mildly afraid of what she could find inside given Carla's history. Maybe she wasn't giving her enough credit, but she often dropped the ball when it came to responsibilities—though a lot of that came from high school- and college-age Carla.

Fortunately, as far as Claire could tell, no major catastrophes had occurred in her absence. It's not like she could judge, anyway, even if it had. After all, that whole detergent incident happened on her watch. *What can I say? My dog is a menace.*

"Carla?" Claire called as she walked Walt over to the dog bathing area and tethered his leash to a post. Parts of him were still covered in detergent, and he needed a good rinse.

"Hey, there," came Carla's voice from the back of the laundromat near the row of large-capacity dryers. "That was quick! I'll be right there. I was finishing up with my stuff back here."

"Has it been quiet?" Claire asked loudly enough for Carla to hear over the thumping of what she assumed to be the dryer balls in her dryer.

"Very. Jet from Cold Brew came in and dropped that stuff over by the washers off—but that's it. He said he was a regular and that you'd know what to do with it. Normal schedule for pickup, he said."

Claire glanced over at the laundry bags resting near the line of washing machines and nodded. Jet worked at the coffee shop in town, and as a musician at night. His unusual schedule made it difficult to get his laundry done on his own—so he had become a regular customer. It also helped that his girlfriend, Morgan, another *Cold Brew* employee, had an apartment right around the corner. He often dropped his clothing off on the way to or from her place.

"Okay, no problem," Claire confirmed as she assessed whether she'd even need dog shampoo for this bath, given the laundry detergent situation. She wasn't thrilled with the idea of *washing* him with the detergent, but... at this point, she didn't think it would really make much of a difference given that he was already covered in it.

Claire figured it was close enough and moved Walt to stand over one of the drains built directly into the floor. Then, she turned on the water, checked the temperature, and began to hose him down with the lukewarm spray. Immediately, soap suds began to rise from the areas of his fur where it had absorbed the detergent. *Nope. No shampoo today.*

After a few moments, Carla emerged from the back area of the laundromat carrying two large laundry bags over her shoulders. "Done!" she said, glancing at Walt who looked pathetic under the stream of water as Claire rinsed the suds from him. He looked so much smaller with his fur wet.

"You need any help?" Carla asked.

"No. I'm good. He was due for a bath anyway, so no big deal. Not how I would have planned to do this, but... here we are! It's just taking longer than usual to get him rinsed off. There are so many bubbles!" Claire groaned as she underwent what she hoped would be her final rinse. "There. All clean. Now for the fun part," she said, her sarcasm obvious. She winced as she reached for the blow drier that hung on a metal rack beside the bath area.

Walt glared at the dryer and let out a bark, narrowing his eyes. "Oh, Sir Walter, get over it. We go through this every time. You have to get dried or you make the whole place smell like a swampy, wet dog! I realize it's not *your* fault that your breed is stinky when wet—but I *do* have to dry you. A laundromat can't stink!"

"Full conversations with your dog in public, and you wonder why you're still single," Carla said, smirking.

"Excuse me? I'll have you know the vet just gave me his number *and* asked me to text him!"

"Claire, the veterinarian telling you to give him an

17

update on your dog's wellbeing when he's sick doesn't count as a relationship," Carla teased.

"No. He wanted me to text him. To go out sometime. On a date," Claire clarified, elbowing her friend as she turned on the blow dryer.

Carla reached over her shoulder and clicked the dryer off. "Whoa... no. No, no, no, uh-uh. You don't get to reveal something like that and then just return to your merry dog washing responsibilities. Dennis is *CUTE!* You should have told me about this the second you walked in. Spill! Details. Now!"

"There really isn't much to tell. He examined Walt, then gave me his number and told me I could text him—whether it was about the dog or not." She shrugged. For some reason, the situation wasn't giving her the chills she expected. She should be excited, but there were no butterflies over the idea of going out with Dr. Den—*just* Dennis.

"Are you going to text him? Girl, you *have* to text him!" Carla jumped up and down a few times in place, clapping her hands together.

"I might," Claire said calmly. "I'll be sure to let you know if I do, given that you seem to be more excited about my love life than I am."

"No offense, but, at this point it's your *lack* of love life that concerns me. If you do text him, you must tell me how it goes immediately!" Carla demanded.

"Yes, Carla, immediate—"

Before Claire could finish her sentence, the front doors swung open, causing the bell to ring several times. Hearing the bell, Walt, who was still soaking wet thanks to Carla's interrogation, jumped in place, attempted to spin around in a circle, barked a few times, then shook off his fur in several sweeping motions, causing water to splash all over Carla and Claire. They glanced at each other, then at the dog, then at the front door. Claire's jaw dropped for a moment, but she caught herself, hanging the dryer on its rack before it, too, dropped to the ground. She composed herself quickly.

"Carla, stay here with Walt for a second?" she asked quietly, making her way to the front to see what the handsome stranger needed. Carla's jaw had already dropped, and she nodded, struggling to find words.

Having made his way through the front door in a hurry, the man stood by the front counter, arms outstretched in his expensive black suit. His blue-hued eyes were wide with panic, and in one hand, he held a leash with a small dog at the end—a puppy. It looked like some sort of hound mix—perhaps a beagle? It was adorable, and very, *very* excited. Carla stood by the dog baths, trying, with only limited success, to control Walt's excitement at the puppy's presence.

As Claire took in the man more fully, she noticed the large, dark stain on the front of his crisp, white-collared shirt. "Hi, can I help you?" she asked, assuming the stain was probably the issue at hand.

"Hello—hi—yes. I—well, actually—he," gesturing to the puppy, "seems to have managed to spill the contents of my afternoon caffeine intake all over me at a particularly inopportune time." The man laughed, shrugging and glancing down at his dog. "I was just at *Cold Brew on Main,* and they suggested I stop here since it's on the way to my meeting location. They said that someone here named Claire is a miracle worker on stains. I was wondering if she may have a quick fix? This meeting is quite career crucial. I'd rather avoid looking like I don't know how to consume a beverage independently."

Claire bent down and gave the puppy a scratch behind his ears. "Aww, I bet he didn't mean it. Probably was just excited. I think I can help... I'm Claire, laundry extraordinaire, apparently! What's his name?" she gestured to the dog.

The man paused for a moment, grinning. "Chaos," he replied simply. "Trust me, it fits."

Claire smiled, then pointed over at Walt, who was spinning circles around Carla, tangling her up in his leash. Carla gave a weak wave, acknowledging she was *not* the one in control.

"I've got one of those, too. His name is Sir Walter the Bouvier, a title far too distinctive for such a stark raving lunatic. In fact, we just left the vet's office. Long story, but if you take a peek in the office, you'll probably be able to piece together the puzzle. Anyway, let's fix the issue at hand. What shirt size are you? And how much time do you have?" Claire asked.

The man peered at her quizzically. "What?" he asked.

"Well, if your meeting is as soon as you've made it out to be, there's no way I'll be able to get this stain out and dry your shirt that fast, but I have an idea. Now..." Claire snapped her fingers. "Shirt size?"

"Uh, extra-large usually," he said, still confused.

"Perfect! I think, anyway," Claire exclaimed, moving to her office area, slipping her shoes off before entering. The man gave her a strange look. "Don't ask. Had a little detergent situation this morning. It's for the best. Trust me." She entered the half door and made her way around the outskirts of the room until she reached a rack in the back. Pulling a crisp, white-collared shirt off, she glanced at the size—large. *Oh well. Close enough. It'll have to do.* As she walked back to the front, she made a mental note that she would have to replace the shirt or pay her friend back if it didn't make its way back in a reasonable time frame.

"Here," she called as she returned to the front of the building. "Put this on. It may be a bit more fitted on you than the other was, but I think it will work well with that suit." She used the new shirt as an opportunity to look the man up and down. *Oof. Dennis may have been lacking in the area of butterflies, but... holy mother of laundry detergent! This man was not.* She could feel the warmth rising in her cheeks.

"Oh, I couldn't just—"

"Just do it," came Carla's pleading voice from the bathing area. She was, by that point, tangled in Walt's leash entirely, sitting on the floor. The dog was licking her face. "Do it fast. And, Claire, please help?"

"Oh, Carla. I'm so sorry!" Claire, having forgotten about her friend's plight, rushed over and grabbed Walt's leash, untangling it and helping Carla back up. "He was just excited over Chaos being here. I mean, the puppy. Although, he does seem to enjoy bringing chaos wherever he goes, too," she chuckled.

Walking Walt over to one of the spare folding rooms, she closed him inside. "Don't worry, boy. I'll let you back in the office as soon as I get the floor cleaned up."

When Claire walked back up to the front, the still-nameless-to-her man was standing in the same place, holding the shirt up as if deciding what to do.

"Alright, more detailed instructions. I'll hold Chaos. You go try the shirt on. If it fits well enough, bring me the stained one and I'll have it fixed by tomorrow. Possibly later today, depending on how stubborn the fabric is." Claire directed him further, "You can use the washroom in the back—second door on the left." *Although, I certainly*

wouldn't be disappointed if you were to try it on right here...
No, Claire, snap out of it.

"Okay. Okay, thanks. I'm James, by the way."

"Claire," she said, smiling.

"Ahh, yes, the miracle worker herself," he said, making his way toward the washroom.

JAMES

Chapter 4

JAMES STEPPED INTO THE WASHROOM HOLDING the crisp, clean shirt on the hanger. He glanced back to see Claire on her knees playing with Chaos, then lifting him up to snuggle her face into his puppy fur. *He really is the perfect wingman.* He chuckled. *If I were looking for anything like that, that is.*

He removed his suit jacket, draping it carefully over an empty towel rack, then unbuttoned his stained button-down shirt and pulled it from his arms. Finally, he lifted his undershirt over his head, which was also stained and wet.

Hadn't thought about that. Oh well. "I'll have to do with-out," he said to himself as he put his arms through the holes on the new shirt. It was definitely significantly more snug than he was used to, but without the undershirt beneath it, he could get by. It was better than a stained shirt.

Throwing his jacket back on, he glanced in the mirror. *Not bad. Maybe I'll start sizing down all my shirts.* James laughed as he pulled open the door and headed back out to the front to give his original shirt to Claire.

"I can't thank you enough. Now, the second problem to address is—" his voice trailed off as an idea popped into his head. With all the wasted time, he'd been struggling to figure out how he would get Chaos either home or to a friend's house and still make it to his meeting on time. *I wonder if...*

"Hey, so... I hate to even ask this, since we just met, and you've already gone out of your way to be so helpful, but would you be able to keep an eye on Chaos for a couple of hours? Think of him as puppy collateral. I'll bring this shirt back and pick him up after my meeting. And of course, I'll pay you whatever you want for the favor."

Claire smiled. "You got it. I wouldn't turn down a couple of hours playing with a puppy—especially one as cute as Chaos! Aside from Walter's shenanigans, it's been pretty slow around here today. Go to your meeting. I'll be here with Chaos when you get back. Puppysitting is no charge, at least for the first time."

"Oh, no. I'm paying you for your time—but we'll talk about it when I get back." James smiled. "I've gotta get going if I'm going to make it on time. I can't tell you how much you've helped me. I don't trust just anyone with my puppy, you know!" He started for the door, then turned back around. "Oh, here, take my number in case you need to reach me about Chaos while I'm gone." He jotted his number on a piece of a receipt he dug out of his pocket and handed it to Claire.

"Ooh," Carla teased from her side, just loud enough for everyone to hear. "Two numbers in one day? You go, girl!"

Claire elbowed her in the ribs, effectively quieting her. "Shush," she hissed between her teeth.

Pretending he didn't hear Carla, James gave a quick wave and made his way out to the street, where he climbed into his black T-top sports car and took off. It was an expensive car, but he had zero regrets over the high-ticket purchase. It was the only thing he'd ever splurged on for himself—and he'd waited for several promotions and built a hefty enough savings account before doing so. This was one reason he liked going to *Cold Brew* so much. He and the owner of the shop, Ben, could get lost for hours talking about cars. Ben had directed him to Claire to get his shirt fixed, but James found himself wondering, after seeing Claire, if there was another motive. *She is pretty hot—and obviously super kind to help a stranger like this.*

It wasn't that he didn't *want* a girlfriend. James had been so focused on his career over the past several years that he just didn't have time. After a while, it didn't seem particularly important. He'd gone on dates here and there but had always found them lackluster and relatively boring. There was no spark. He felt more of a spark introducing one of his computer systems to a new client than he did talking to most of the women he'd met. Although he had to admit, Claire did have something about her that drew him in and made him curious.

James had actually felt a strange tinge of jealousy—or perhaps just disappointment—at hearing her friend say she'd been given another man's phone number that day, without even knowing the circumstances. It was silly. They didn't even know each other. Still, he couldn't deny that she was someone he may *want* to know, depending on how this meeting went, anyway. If he was moving across the country, none of it really mattered, did it?

James walked into the large office building and took the elevator to the 4th floor, then entered one of the office suites.

"Hello," he greeted the receptionist. "James Dorland here to see Mr. Marzini, please. We have a meeting." The woman behind the desk was polished and precise, her sharp bob framing a face that was both welcoming and assessing. "Oh, Mr. Dorland, nice to see you in person. I'm Bridget, Mr. Marzini's Executive Assistant. We spoke several times on the phone. He is just finishing up a conference call. I'll let him know you're here. Can I get you anything in the meantime? Coffee? Water? Tea?"

"No, thank you. I've had enough close encounters with coffee for one day," he said, smiling.

"What?" she asked, confused.

"Oh, nothing. Nevermind. I'm good, thanks."

She shook it off and plastered a smile across her face. "Alright, Mr. Dorland, have a seat. I'll let you know when he is ready for you."

James took a seat in the reception area of *T.M. Enterprises,* one of the country's largest cloud computing tech companies, among many other areas of tech. As a cloud computing architect and consultant, James had spent the past several years designing and implementing strategies for large companies and organizations. Most people had no idea what that even meant, so he usually just told people he was in computer consulting.

Now, he had the opportunity to move into the executive side as the V.P. of Infrastructure for *T.M. Enterprises*. It was a big jump, but one for which he'd been preparing for a long time. Having by-passed the typical interview process through word-of-mouth in the industry, he was recruited to meet directly with the CEO to discuss the role and whether he'd be a good fit. As he sat in the luxe office, he began to wonder whether he could actually pull this off!

In an attempt to curb his anxiety, James let his mind wander freely, finding himself revisiting the events of earlier that day—the coffee spill, and the woman at the laundromat and her big, wet dog. For a moment, he wondered if he was crazy, leaving his puppy with a complete stranger. Claire certainly didn't *feel* like a stranger, though. She seemed... comfortable, almost as if he'd known her his entire life. Not to mention, very attractive!

"Mr. Dorland, Mr. Marzini is ready for you. I'll show you in." Bridget's voice intruded on his thoughts, taking him by surprise. James cleared his throat as he rose to his feet, preparing for the most important meeting of his life thus far. It had the potential to set his career trajectory in a whole new direction. Still, somehow, he could only think about one thing... and it *definitely* wasn't work-related.

Bridget led James down a long hallway to a private elevator that required a code for access. After they entered, she punched in several numbers, and the elevator door closed, taking them up several floors. When the doors opened, he found himself staring into a massive office decorated in modern black, white, and gray. Like the décor, the space was uncluttered and minimalistic, with few office supplies lying about—a rarely used space. It made sense. James knew it wasn't Mr. Marzini's primary office and assumed it was mainly used for meetings during his business trips to the region.

Bridget stepped from the elevator first, knocking gently on the entry area paneling to indicate their presence. "Knock, knock," she cooed. The high-backed office chair on the far side of the space spun around slowly away from the window overlooking the park below, to face the desk it was set behind. A tall, polished man in his mid-fifties rose to his feet.

"Ahh, Mr. Dorland, a pleasure to finally meet you in person. I'm Tom, Tom Marzini," he introduced himself with a broad grin, gesturing to James to enter further.

James took several steps across the room, closing the space between him and Mr. Marzini, as Bridget left via the elevator. He stretched an arm out toward the CEO, inviting him to shake his hand. "A pleasure to meet you, Sir," he said.

"The pleasure is mine. I've heard good things about you, Dorland. Very good things. I think you'd make a solid addition to the *T.M. Enterprises* team. Sit down. We've got a lot to talk about."

"Thank you, Sir," James said as he sat in the chair set in front of the large desk, facing Mr. Marzini, who sat in his desk chair, resting his elbows on the table and folding his hands before him.

"Please, call me Tom. So... Before we go any further, how do you feel about Santa Clara, California?"

"It's on the opposite side of the country," James responded without thinking.

"Indeed. It is. And it's the cloud computing capital of the world!"

Making Introductions

CLAIRE

Chapter 5

"HE OBVIOUSLY LIKES YOU," CARLA ARGUED. "HE left his *dog* with you for Heaven's sake!"

"As collateral," Claire pointed out.

"For a *shirt*, Claire. You don't trade your dog for a shirt," she said, rolling her eyes. "He was looking for a reason to come back!"

"He wasn't *trading* his dog, Carla. He just needed a favor. And you know me, I don't know how to say no..." Her voice trailed off. *Especially to handsome businessmen in sexy suits.*

"Yeah, okay. You can honestly tell me that you're not waiting with bated breath for him to come back so you can see him again?"

"Only because I don't have time to watch a needy puppy all day," Claire lied.

As if on cue, Chaos let out a whine from the office where Claire had left him after cleaning up the massive detergent mess. Despite her initial refusal to help remedy the detergent disaster, Carla assisted by keeping an eye on Chaos during the massive undertaking.

"But it's a really cute puppy, though." Carla gestured to the half wall, peering at the dog as he explored the new territory, sniffing every square inch of the room. "And his owner isn't half bad, either!"

"Carla, you're *married!*"

"I meant for you," she chuckled. "Although, if Matty wouldn't mind a third..."

"New topic!" Claire announced. "Don't you have somewhere to be or something? Your comforters have been finished for over an hour now..."

"Oh, come on. I missed you, girl. Can you blame a girl for wanting to spend some quality time with one of her besties?" Carla wiggled her eyebrows.

"So, this has absolutely nothing to do with wanting to be here when *he* comes back for Chaos so you can play your favorite game?"

Carla feigned innocence. "I have no idea what you're talking about!"

"Matchmaker, Carla. Gia. Ben. Ringing any bells?" Claire asked, referring to the integral role Carla had played in getting her friend back together with her high school sweetheart.

"Listen, that was *all* them. All I did was push things

along a bit." She grinned, clearly immensely pleased with her efforts and the way everything had worked out for Gia and Ben.

"Yeah, sure it was. Well, regardless, I need to get some work done at some point today. I'm going to bring Walt into the office to introduce him to Chaos, then, hopefully, fold some of the wash-and-fold items if they get along. I have a few people picking up later this evening." Claire glanced at the line of tall laundry bags stacked against the wall, each containing washed but still unfolded clothing.

"Walt has never met a dog he didn't like. I don't think they'll have a problem together." Carla sighed. "Fine. I guess I'll leave you to it, but you better text me the second he leaves and tell me how it went!"

"How *what* went? Picking up his dog? I imagine everything will go just fine..."

"You know exactly what I mean—and I want details." Carla scoffed as she grabbed the large bags that held her blankets and hefted them over her shoulder.

"You're impossible, Carla."

"I know. Text me."

After Carla left, Claire glanced over the half wall at Chaos. He had found a dog toy long ago forgotten by Walt and was tossing it high in the air, then chasing it in a game of solo fetch. Claire chuckled. *He really is a cute puppy.*

"Good thing Walt is good at sharing," Claire told the dog, making her way to the back of the laundromat to release Walt from the confines of the room where she'd been keeping him while she cleaned up the detergent spill.

She opened the door and moved aside, allowing Walt to do his bear-run toward the office, still monitoring his movements to be sure his mobility was alright after the events of earlier in the day. When he reached the half-door, he jumped up in his trademark two paws on the door position, peering at the smaller dog in the office. His tail was wagging enthusiastically and he showed no signs of aggression, so she went about preparing the two to interact. Walt was very well socialized to people and dogs, so she wasn't too concerned, but it was always better safe than sorry—especially since Chaos was still so small. Not to mention the fact that she barely knew his owner, and it seemed like he'd have the means to hire a decent attorney should something go awry.

Claire clipped Walt to his leash, which she tied to a strong metal ring attached to the half door. She used it to keep him in one place when the laundromat got busy. She scooped Chaos up in her arms, removed the toy he had been playing with from the area, picked up the food and water bowls, and relocated anything else that could trigger toy or resource guarding. Not that Walt had ever exhibited this, but again, safety first.

Finally, Claire opened the half-door and walked over to the desk, sitting with Chaos in her lap. Still leashed to the door, Walt exhibited a curious excitement as Claire rolled the wheeled chair a little closer, allowing both dogs to catch a whiff of the other's scent. Immediately, Walt moved into a gentle play bow—a good sign. Both dogs seemed relaxed and comfortable. Still, Claire kept them distanced as she completed some paperwork at her desk.

Finally, she scooted the chair back over to Walt and allowed him and Chaos to interact directly for the first time. After several minutes, she was convinced that they were curious about each other but noted no aggression. Unclipping Walt's leash from the door, she commanded him to sit and stay (using his full name, of course) while she placed Chaos down at her feet. The two sniffed each other several times. Then, to Claire's surprise, Walt rolled over into a submissive, belly-up position with his legs in the air.

Claire couldn't help but laugh at the sight of this large, adult dog rolling over and submitting to such a tiny little pup. "Well, then... I guess we know who the boss is around here." She grinned at Chaos, then snapped a picture with her phone. She stared at it for a moment, then—before she could overthink it—sent it to James with the caption: *Your dog has already taken over. Walt never stood a chance.*

The reply came faster than she expected.

James Shirt: *Like owner, like dog.*

She stared at the three dots that appeared, then disappeared, then appeared again.

James Shirt: *That sounded smoother in my head. What I meant was, Chaos has a way of winning people over. Clearly a family trait.*

Claire bit her lip to keep from smiling and set the phone face-down on the desk. *Do not read into this. He's being friendly. People are friendly. It's a thing.*

She stared at the phone for a full thirty seconds. Then, before she could second-guess herself, she picked it back up.

Claire: *You should come to Yappy Hour. Two weeks from now. Dogs, raffles, community chaos. Your kind of scene.*

Her thumb hovered over the send button. She added one more line.

Claire: *If you're going to be in town long enough.*

She frowned at her own wording. *What does that even mean?* She hit send anyway.

James Shirt: *I wouldn't miss it. Chaos and I will be there with bells on.*

James Shirt: *Not literal bells. He'd eat them.*

Claire laughed out loud. *Okay. That was smooth.*

As the two dogs became more familiar with each other,

Claire felt more comfortable giving them a bit more space. She was able to do almost all the folding as they tumbled around, ran circles through the office, then finally collapsed in a pile with Walt on the bottom to take a nap—another photo opportunity. She sent that one too, and James responded with a string of heart-eye emojis that made her feel things she immediately filed under "to be dealt with later."

The entire time, Claire kept her eye on the door, greeting self-serve laundry clients as they came and went and awaiting James' return. She had to admit she was excited to show him how well the two pets were getting along.

By the time Claire finished folding the wash-and-fold, another hour had passed. She couldn't imagine James would be much longer, but she didn't like wasting time, so she set about the next task on her to-do list. *Ugh. Yappy Hour. Event planning.*

Claire loved her customers and their pets, and her most recent passion project was aimed at building a larger clientele for the dog wash portion of the laundromat, helping local animal shelters, *and* fostering a stronger community. Thus far, things were generally quiet on the dog wash front, and the revenue hadn't even come close to paying for the improvements she'd made for the business venture. Sure, she had some regular customers, but if she was honest, the entire business wasn't doing all that great.

She had gone into the endeavor with a limited marketing budget, but to spread the word, Claire had come up with the idea of *Yappy Hour.* She planned to launch the monthly dog-friendly community meet-up at the park across the street in about two weeks. She hoped it would lead to support for another of her ideas—transforming a long-neglected portion of the park into a dog park, which, ideally, would lead to more dog wash customers who didn't want to bring muddy, slobber-covered dogs home after a frolicking with their canine friends.

Opening her laptop, Claire started drafting emails to nearby businesses she hadn't yet contacted, hoping to get a few extra item donations for raffles and the gift bags she was creating for attendees. She couldn't keep herself from glancing at the door every few minutes, wondering when James would return.

Return Customer

JAMES

Chapter 6

"HELL YEAH!" JAMES SHOUTED AS HE EXITED THE *T.M. Enterprises* building, raising his arm up, then pulling it quickly back down, bent at the elbow in a victory motion. He had been expecting tough questions, a challenge to his skills, or to be flat-out rejected over his lack of administrative or executive experience. Instead, he felt like he'd been welcomed to join the company with open arms, offered an extremely competitive salary and benefits package, and was practically begged to take the job.

James always felt like he wasn't enough. No matter how

much success came his way, he expected the bottom to drop out at any minute. He hoped things would be different this time. With a title like "Vice President," perhaps his family would finally take him seriously. Working from home, they'd always implied he didn't have a "real job," even though he made more money than either of them did at their nine-to-fives. They couldn't stand that he worked the hours that were best for him—and that sometimes it was 2 am.

Maybe they would finally see why he wasn't settled down, married, with two kids and a dog. Well, actually, speaking of dogs, he *did* have one now... and, indirectly, his parents were the reason he got Chaos, so he was grateful for that. He'd hoped it would stop their nagging about him being so *alone* all the time. *I do have friends, you know!* But he had to admit, Chaos had brought him a great deal of joy in the short time he'd had him—not to mention an excuse to go back to the laundromat...

No, no, no. Now is NOT the time to be thinking about a woman! James told himself, groaning. He was about to commit to moving just about as far across the country as physically possible for a job opportunity. He shook his head a few times, acknowledging the absurdity, as he made his way to his car to pick up Chaos and swap shirts. *I haven't been interested in anyone for how long? I'm going to start now!?* He rolled his eyes. *No. Absolutely not.*

Claire

Claire glanced at the door again, just in time to see James walking up to the entrance. If it were even possible, he looked more attractive than the first time he had come in. He still wore his suit pants but had removed his tie and unbuttoned a few buttons on his collar. He held his jacket casually tucked under one arm. The snug-fitting white button-up sleeves were rolled up just past his elbows, showing several tattoos on his forearms. *Unexpected,* Claire thought. The shirt accentuated the natural contours of his body, showing off his athletic build. The look could be described as fashionably disheveled—and extremely sexy.

As he walked through the front door, the bell rang, causing both dogs to abandon their nap pile and erupt into a frenzy of barked greetings.

"Whoa, there," James began. "It seems the canines have been introduced. How's everyone getting along?" James asked, smiling at Claire as she opened the half door and slid out past both dogs. Walt jumped up, taking his usual position to gaze out into the rest of the laundromat.

"Incredibly well, actually! It seems that little Chaos is in charge, though. He's been keeping Sir Walt in line," Claire said with a chuckle. "They've been playing and napping in spurts all afternoon."

James walked over to the half door and gave Walt a scratch behind the ears before gazing down at Chaos, who was too short to reach even halfway up the door.

"Thanks for taking care of my little guy," James said. Claire smiled in response, not entirely sure whether he was talking to her or Walt. "And thanks for the shirt," he added, turning to look directly at Claire. "It was truly a lifesaver—well, a career saver anyway."

"Oh, no problem at all. Anytime," Claire responded awkwardly, recognizing that the odds of this particular situation happening 'another time' were slim to none.

"I bought a t-shirt on the way back, in case my shirt wasn't salvageable. I can give the borrowed one back and just throw this one on." As he spoke, he rolled his sleeves back down and began unbuttoning the shirt he was wearing.

"Oh, uh, okay," Claire sputtered, trying to avert her eyes from his chest as James removed the shirt entirely, then quickly pulled the black t-shirt over his head. *For the love of all things holy, he looks even better in a black t-shirt than he did in the suit.*

She coughed, trying to compose herself, then continued, "It's definitely a stain I can get out. Coffee isn't so bad. Not like red wine or grass stains. I can get those too, but they take a bit more work." Claire could feel herself pouring out word vomit. *So many unnecessary words!*

"I just... with the dogs here to watch and some other things I had to handle at the same time, I didn't get a chance to focus on it while you were gone. I'm happy to return it as-is." *He doesn't need to know that I actually got so distracted by the dogs and the event planning that I completely forgot about the stain.*

"How about if I come back tomorrow? And, I have a confession to make..."

"What's that?" Claire asked, hoping her face wasn't as beet red as it felt.

"Don't get mad, but I usually just throw out a shirt once I spill something on it—which seems to happen surprisingly often for someone with as much poise and grace as me," he joked. "Sadly, not everyone is as charmed as you are in the stain removal department." He rubbed his chin thoughtfully, then added, "In fact, I'd love a brief stain-fighting tutorial tomorrow, if you have the time."

"Of course. I'm free anytime except around lunchtime. I have a *Yappy Hour* meeting."

"Ahh, the event you texted me about! I'm looking forward to it. Chaos and I wouldn't miss it."

"Good! Oh, that reminds me—one sec," Claire said as she slinked back through the half door, using her hip to block Walt from escaping. She scooped Chaos up in her arms, then grabbed a flier from the stack on her desk before deciding to take a small pile. *He probably knows a lot of people...*

Coming out of the office, Claire handed James the fliers listing the time, date, location, and other event information. "If you know anyone who may be interested, feel free to pass these along. I'm trying to make this a monthly thing, but we'll see how it goes the first time around, I guess." She smiled, then handed Chaos to him, fetching his leash. Chaos nuzzled into James' neck in greeting, and he returned the gesture with a few gentle kisses against his fur.

Something about a man and a puppy. Oof! Calm down, Claire.

Claire clipped the leash onto his collar.

"So, are we on for tomorrow?" James asked. "A quick laundry lesson?"

She smiled. "Sure. You got it. Before 11 or after 1, I'll be here. Feel free to bring Chaos. Walter would love to play with him again, I'm sure. And if you want, I can show you how the dog washing stations work. Trust me, with a puppy, you never know when one might come in handy. Although, I'm pretty much always here to help, anyway."

"Chaos and I will be there. Thank you so much for everything, Claire. It's been a pleasure meeting you. We look forward to seeing you again tomorrow—and Walter, of course."

Ugh, that killer smile again. "Likewise," Claire said, trying to keep her cool even though she felt like melting right then and there.

"Oh," James added. "I almost forgot!" He dug deep into his pocket and fished out his wallet. Pulling out a wad of bills, he peeled several off and smoothed them out, handing them to Claire.

"Oh, it's really not necess—whoa! I think you've made a mistake. This is five hundred dollars! *Definitely* not necessary," Claire mumbled, finding the words difficult to form in her state of shock.

"You literally saved my ass today. You have no idea. Consider it a pre-payment for laundry lessons, if it makes you more comfortable. I've got a lot to learn, I promise!" Before Claire had a chance to pass the money back or object any further, James had turned and bolted to the door with Chaos.

Before he escaped, she shouted, "This is too much! I still have your number, you know! I can still get in touch with you!"

"I sincerely hope you do," he yelled. "Feel free to call or text later to continue this discussion—but I'm not taking it back. Either way, I will see you tomorrow!"

Claire glanced down at the cash in her hand, then over at Walter. Five hundred dollars. That was the repairman for Machine 3. Two weeks of utilities. Half the insurance payment she'd been strategically ignoring.

Her fingers tightened around the bills.

She walked into the office slowly and stared at the broken dryer note still highlighted in green on her list. Green meant money. She could fix the machine. She could breathe for a month. She could stop calculating every dollar before it left her hand.

Instead, she exhaled and walked to the large plastic jar on her desk labeled *Dog Park Donations*.

"If I start treating kindness like an emergency fund," she muttered to Walt, "I become someone I don't like."

She slid the money into the jar. Then she paused. Then she pulled one bill back out.

"One repair," she told Walt firmly. "We can't host Yappy Hour with a broken dryer."

The rest stayed in the jar. She stepped back.

"Investment," she corrected herself. "Not charity."

She glanced at the door James had disappeared through. For the first time in a long time, something in her chest felt awake. That was dangerous. Because things that wake up can also leave.

Pig Dreams

JAMES

Chapter 7

JAMES STROLLED TO HIS CAR, OPENED THE
passenger side door, and placed Chaos down before walking
to the other side and climbing in himself. "Five hundred
dollars?! I must be crazy... What is this woman doing to
me?!"

He placed his head between his hands and groaned.
Better be some damn good laundry lessons. He shifted the car
into reverse and pulled out of his parking spot. "Chaos, you
need to be socialized anyway, right? I guess the laundro-
mat/dog wash is as good a place as any to start," he said,

shaking his head. "For the bargain price of five hundred dollars."

As James drove through his neighborhood, he felt a knot form in his stomach. The tree-lined streets and well-kept sidewalks were inviting—the kind of neighborhood where people left their porch lights on and waved from their driveways. He passed the bakery on Main Street where the owner, Rosa, always saved him a bear claw on Wednesdays. He passed the park where he ran with Chaos every morning, the one with the fountain that the local kids used as a wading pool in the summer. He passed the hardware store where old Mr. Fredrickson gave unsolicited life advice along with incorrect change. It was a place that had somehow, without him noticing, stopped being temporary. And it wouldn't be easy to leave this all behind. He had bought his house at just the right time—and it would sell for a significant profit—but somehow, the idea of moving across the country still stung. Not only was it his first house, but it was the only place he had ever really felt "at home." As a kid, he moved around a lot with his parents as they focused on advancing their careers. Now, working remotely, he'd spent more time here than anywhere else he'd lived over the past several years, and probably his entire lifetime.

For the first time since the potentially life-changing meeting ended, James felt conflicted. He knew he couldn't throw away such an amazing career opportunity, but how could he leave this place? It felt like such an important crossroads. Bittersweet, nonetheless. He wished there were a way to take on the VP role while remaining local. He'd worked remotely for the better part of his adult life... why wouldn't he be able to pull it off in this position? Suddenly, he felt an overwhelming compulsion to stay, but he pushed the desires down deep. He'd worked his entire life for this opportunity. He knew he couldn't just throw it away.

Not just to stay in his home. There would be another home out in California. Just as nice, probably nicer. Career first, like always. He tried to focus on the many possibilities he would have out in California with a new title and a new life.

"At least you'll be coming with me, right, buddy?" James reached over and tousled Chaos's fur. "We'll be good. We have each other. That's all we need, right?"

Then, his phone buzzed. He pulled it out, and a wide grin spread across his face. He leaned back into his car seat to respond before heading inside.

Claire

Later that evening, Claire lay stretched out on her bed, still buzzing from the day's chaos. *I can't believe I texted him first. Or at all. I never do that!* She glanced down at the words on the screen of her phone and smiled at the name that popped up: James Shirt. It was the title she'd assigned him in her phone. She'd forgotten his last name somehow, if he'd even given it.

Claire: You gave me too much money.

James Shirt: I gave you just enough... for dog sitting and laundry lessons!

Claire: You're impossible.

James Shirt: You have no idea. See you tomorrow! I expect a well-thought-out lesson on the ins and outs of coffee stain removal.

Claire: I'm your girl! For $500, you get all my secrets. See you and Chaos then.

Did I really just say, "I'm your girl?" Ugh. She groaned as she set her phone down. Within moments, another notification popped up. Expecting it to be James again, she quickly grabbed and unlocked the screen.

Dr. Dennis: Hi Claire, I wanted to check on Walter. How's he doing?

Claire chuckled. *Was that today?* The fiasco with Walter and the detergent felt like it had happened days ago, honestly. He was acting like his normal, crazy self throughout his puppy playdate, so she'd practically forgotten about the chaos earlier that morning.

Claire: Hi, Dr. Dennis. Thanks for checking in. Walt seems just fine. Maybe a little embarrassed about the whole thing, but that's about it.

Dr. Dennis: Just Dennis, remember? I'm glad he's okay! How would you feel about a follow-up appointment... maybe in the park with coffee?

Claire: Interesting choice of location for a veterinary appointment, just Dennis, but I'm open-minded! I'm in. Tomorrow?

Claire chuckled at herself. She knew he was hitting on her, and she decided to let him. After all, he *was* a great guy. He was cute, funny, and she missed someone flirting with her. So, she went with it. Still, she wished it were James she was meeting in the park. Sure, they'd be having their laundry lesson the next day, but Claire had no reason to believe James had any further interest in her than having cleaner clothes and a convenient puppy-sitter.

Dennis: Perfect. I'm not exactly sure what time yet. I have a full schedule in the morning, but maybe I will have a cancellation, or we can do some time in the afternoon. Can we confirm tomorrow?

Claire: Sure. I'll talk to you tomorrow!

Claire placed the phone on the nightstand beside her. She didn't mean to cut their conversation short, but she felt utterly exhausted. Between the normal workday responsibilities, the detergent fiasco, an unexpected trip to the vet, a bath for Walt, and an unanticipated puppy play date, the day had felt unnaturally *long*. It was early, but she didn't anticipate she'd have any trouble falling asleep under the circumstances, so she gave in and pulled her legs up at the knees to tuck them beneath the blankets. Her excitement over seeing both Dennis and James the next day was nothing in comparison to how tired she was, and within minutes, her eyelids felt heavy, then she was fast asleep.

The next morning, Claire's alarm blared, pulling her out of the sweetest little dream. The details felt a little foggy, but it took place at the dog park she'd been envisioning for months. It was perfect—and just as she'd imagined it would look. She was there with Walt and a man, although she couldn't quite figure out who it was. It was almost as if his features were hidden in shadow. Dream Claire didn't seem to notice, though.

There didn't seem to be any real point to the dream. It didn't even have a plot! It was essentially just a montage of Claire and this mystery man wandering the park, acting like the perfect couple! He held her hand as dogs of all different breeds frolicked around them, bought her an ice cream from the ice cream truck, and they kissed beneath a large tree in the park. Honestly, it was cheesy as fuck, Claire admitted to herself. Still, somehow it made her feel all mushy inside.

She sighed deeply. *Well, if I didn't want a boyfriend before, I certainly do now.* Claire pushed her blankets back and kicked her legs around and over the side of her bed, rolling her eyes. *It was a sweet dream, though.* She raised her arms above her head in a deep stretch, first to one side, then the other, and as the sleep left her more fully, she remembered that she was supposed to be meeting with two different men that day.

Hello, anxiety! What was I thinking?! She groaned and put her head in her hands. Walt, hearing her stir, lumbered into the bedroom with the urgency of a dog who had been waiting approximately forever for someone to acknowledge his existence. He placed his chin on the edge of the bed and stared at her with liquid brown eyes that communicated, in order: hunger, love, and mild judgment.

"Don't look at me like that," Claire told him. "You don't have to choose between two men today."

Walt sneezed on her pillow.

"Great. Thanks for that." She wiped the pillow with the edge of her sheet and rose from the bed, stumbling over to her closet. "I have work, a meeting, laundry lessons, and a park date... if it's even a date. And I have absolutely no idea what to wear."

She pulled out three different tops, held each one against herself in the mirror, rejected all of them, then pulled them out again and repeated the process. The first was too casual. The second was too try-hard. The third had a stain on the collar that she—a professional stain remover—had somehow missed.

"Ironic," she muttered, tossing it in the hamper.

She settled on a fitted navy V-neck that she'd owned for years and a pair of jeans that Carla once described as "the only pair you own that acknowledges you have a body." Hair down, minimal makeup, sneakers because she had things to do today that didn't involve impractical footwear.

She looked at her reflection. *This is me. Take it or leave it.*

Walt, apparently satisfied with her wardrobe selection, headed toward the kitchen and his food bowl. Claire followed, already mentally organizing her day into manageable blocks. Laundromat from eight to noon. Yappy Hour planning meeting with Tina at one. Dennis at the park sometime in between. James and Chaos in the afternoon for laundry lessons.

Four things. I can do four things. People do four things all the time.

Her stomach disagreed.

Laundry Lessons

JAMES

Chapter 8

JAMES TORE THROUGH HIS CLOSET WITH RECKLESS abandon. "Why didn't I just take the damn shirt and leave?" he mumbled to himself as he searched for something to wear. He couldn't just leave Claire hanging after he said he'd be there today, but he didn't expect to feel so nervous going into their "laundry appointment." He still couldn't figure out why he hadn't just taken his dog back and walked away.

"She bewitched me," he said, chuckling to himself. Finally, he decided on a pair of dark wash jeans and a nice,

50

dark gray t-shirt. After dressing, he stood in front of the full-length mirror on the back of the door of the master bathroom. *Decent, but casual enough to look like I'm not trying too hard.* He face-palmed himself. *I don't know why I'm trying at all. I'm NOT trying... I'm... Fuck. I'm totally trying.*

James sighed as he finished getting ready. They hadn't really set a time other than before 11 or after 1, so James figured he would stop by *Cold Brew on Main* for a cup of coffee, then swing by the laundromat at around ten. *An hour should be good enough for a laundry lesson, right?* He laughed at himself, wondering who would even suggest such a thing in the age of YouTube. He could easily take laundry lessons from the comfort of his own home or *anywhere* with the smart device that was eternally glued to his hand, it seemed.

James pulled his black sneakers on and scooped Chaos up into his arms, nuzzling his puppy's soft fur. "I know, I know. Let's be real, James. This is about the girl," he admitted to his dog, pulling his phone out from his pocket. "Not laundry."

James: Do you drink coffee?

Claire: I do. Unlike you, who wears it as a fashion statement.

James laughed out loud. *Smartass.*

James: If you're going to be a wise ass, I won't bring you any...

Claire: Do you think you can manage to carry two at the same time? *One* didn't go so well for you yesterday.

He grinned. Claire was feisty, and he liked it. Sarcasm was his second language, and it seemed like she wouldn't have a hard time keeping up with his dry wit.

James: Somehow, I'll find a way. And, if not, at least I

know a girl who can get the stains out. What would you like?

Claire: Iced Macchiato, please, and thank you!

James: You got it. See you soon. First coffee, then laundry.

Claire: Sounds good.

James was surprised by how comfortable it felt texting Claire. Almost like he'd known her much longer than, well, a single day. He could get used to talking to her like this, even if it was just as friends—under the circumstances.

Claire

Wait, did this stain-fighting session just become a coffee date? Do I have two dates scheduled today? Are either of them even actual dates?! Claire asked herself a flurry of questions as she pulled a load of laundry from a dryer and tossed it into a rolling laundry cart to bring back into her office to fold. She honestly wasn't sure of the actual answer. *I didn't even know I was IN the dating pool... now I'm drowning in dog-loving men. Or I'm just completely off base, and one simply cares about my dog's wellbeing, while the other wants to become a laundry wizard.*

As she rolled her cart in through the half door, Walter rose from his bed and sauntered over, looking for affection. "Hey there, Walt. This is all your fault, Pupper. I hope you're happy." Walter glanced up at Claire with wide eyes, then licked his wet tongue up the side of her cheek. "That was... appreciated," Claire chuckled. "So, are you in the mood for some Chaos? The little dog, that is—not the insanity *you're* usually causing."

She scratched her dog behind his ears, then began folding the pants before her. Several regular customers were in and out while she worked, but no one with whom she spoke regularly. Over the years, Claire learned that some people want to chat while they do their laundry and others just want to get in, get their items into a machine, and get out quickly, with as little small talk as possible. Just as she was finishing the last pair, the bell on the door rang, indicating someone had entered.

Claire glanced out through the half-door of the office just in time to see James struggling to enter, holding a cardboard tray of two iced coffees as Chaos twisted his leash around his ankles. She jumped up quickly and rushed to the front, grabbing the tray from James.

Claire safely deposited the beverage tray on top of the change machine and squatted at James' feet, untangling Chaos's leash. She raised her face to look at him and smirked.

"Looking to revisit yesterday's chain of events?" she teased, surprising even herself with how smooth she seemed.

"I thought I'd give us some extra coffee stains to combat. You know, just for kicks," he joked. "You foiled my plan by swooping in and rescuing me—again."

"Trust me, I've got enough stains to handle in this place to keep us busy all day and night. I mean, not that you'd be here all day and night or anything. Just for a little while, uh, until you have to leave, or want to leave... until the lesson is over... Uh, you know what I mean." Claire's words tumbled out in a graceless heap. She rose to her feet after giving Chaos a pat on the head, shaking it off.

James' eyes lit up as he watched Claire stumble over her words. Finally, when the awkwardness was too much to take, he handed her the iced coffee. "Iced Macchiato for the laundry wizard," he said. "Breathe."

Claire took the drink from him, raising her eyes to glance at the front door as the bell rang again. Claire's eyes widened. There, standing in the doorway, was Dr. Dennis. He was holding a tray with two cups of *Cold Brew on Main* coffee in it.

"Dr. Den—

"Just Dennis," he corrected. "Someday you'll get it right," he said with the flash of his very toothy, very white smile. "I know I didn't text first, but I took a chance that you'd have a bit of time and brought you an iced—oh."

His face fell somewhat as his eyes caught the cup of coffee in her hand, and, at the same time, noticed James also held a cup from *Cold Brew.* He glanced down at the tray in his hand.

"Guess my timing is off," he chuckled. "Didn't I just see you chatting with Ben in the coffee shop?" Dennis asked James.

"You did, indeed. We have the same car. We like to gush about it to each other like little schoolgirls from time to time," James explained, causing Dennis to shift his weight uncomfortably. Everyone in town knew about the fancy, expensive sports car Ben drove. He wasn't a flashy guy, but it was his pride and joy!

"Ahh, nice," Dennis stated flatly, still holding the tray of drinks.

"We were just about to start a... well, a laundry lesson. I mean, not that James can't do his own laundry... It's more like... Advanced Stain Fighting," Claire stumbled over her words, swooping in to change the subject. She wasn't doing anything wrong by way of either man. Still, she couldn't help feeling a slight tinge of guilt over making plans with both of them on the same day without solidifying the timing with either one. Had she been clearer on her availability, she could have avoided this painfully awkward series of interactions.

"You're offering laundry lessons now, too?" Dennis asked.

"Sort of," Claire began.

"I'm her very first client," James jumped in, lifting Chaos—who was trying to climb his leg—off the floor and holding him against his chest.

"Cute little guy," Dennis said, smiling. "What's his name?"

"Chaos," James replied. "Appropriately named, I might add." He held Chaos out to Dennis in greeting just as Walt jumped up on the half door, spotting his new puppy friend. Walt began whining and scratching at the door in earnest, trying to get to him.

"Dr. Dennis is Sir Walt's veterinarian. The best in town!" Claire said, speaking over Walt's ruckus and trying to smooth over the situation with praise.

Dennis grinned. "One of the *only* ones in town, but I'll take it." He walked over to the door and began petting Walter's head and neck, telling him what a good boy he was. *He really is a good guy,* thought Claire as she watched him interact with her beloved dog.

For a while, no one said anything. James stood, sipping his coffee and petting Chaos as the lull in conversation became almost unbearable. Finally, Dennis made his exit. "Well, I guess it's time I let you get on with your... laundry lesson. Feel free to shoot me a text when you're free, Claire. I'd still love to see you later. I'll leave the coffee in case you want it... later." He shrugged, gave a weak smile, and moved to leave the building.

"Dating?" asked James, glancing toward the door as it closed, ringing the bell.

"Huh?" Claire said, flustered. "No. Just... we're just friends. We went to school together—and he's Walter's vet." Claire wasn't sure why she couldn't admit they had a date scheduled for that day, but for whatever reason, the words didn't come out.

James nodded, chuckling. "Okay, well, let's get this show on the road. Teach me your ways, oh great laundry guru. Should I put Chaos in the office with Walt?"

"Yeah, they've waited long enough. Let them play a bit!"

James lifted Chaos over the half-door, placing him gently onto the floor on the other side. Claire was impressed by how his height allowed him to reach right over the barrier, causing his shirt to cling to his well-formed body closely with the stretch. *Oof.*

The moment the puppy was safely on the ground, Walter rolled onto his back and raised his legs into the air, displaying his stomach in a show of submission. Both James and Claire laughed. "No question who the boss is," Claire said, giggling as they watched their dogs greet each other happily.

"They get along so well," James mused, taking in their interactions.

"I know. They were best buddies from the minute I put them together!"

"Amazing! Okay, so, laundry witch... where do we start?" James took a long sip of his iced coffee, finishing it and tossing it into a nearby trash can.

"Coffee."

"We just did that," James glanced down at his empty cup in the garbage.

"No. Coffee *stains*," Claire clarified. "Yours, in particular. Hang on, let me get your shirt from yesterday."

Cleaning Cocktail

CLAIRE

Chapter 9

AS CLAIRE WALKED TOWARD THE BACK OF THE laundromat, where, presumably, the shirt he'd stained yesterday had been left, James couldn't keep his eyes from traveling the length of her body, taking in her curves. As soon as he caught himself—and before Claire noticed his wandering gaze—he whipped his head around to watch Chaos and Sir Walter, who were in a tug-of-war with a rope toy.

The scene before him was comical enough to elicit a chuckle. Walter, much larger in stature, appeared to be letting Chaos win the battle—or at least going easy on the puppy. Every so often, Walt would release the toy, sending Chaos flying backward with his prize, only to return to repeat the activity.

"Tug of war?" Claire asked, calling out from the back of the laundromat.

"Yeah. They're hilarious."

"I know. I watched them do this for way longer than I had time for yesterday," Claire called back, walking back toward the front. "Okay. I've got our first victim!" She held up the coffee-stained shirt from the day before. "Time for laundry lessons!"

Claire walked over to one of the tables in the center of the laundromat and placed the shirt down flat on top of it, smoothing the fabric. "Now... I probably should have treated this yesterday. One of the first rules of stain fighting is to act fast. The longer it sits, the more it sets." She grinned at James. "It's like regret... but for fabric."

"Will it still come out even after setting?" James asked.

"You're learning from the best of the best," Claire said, squaring her shoulders. "That stain doesn't stand a chance against me!" James chuckled, appreciating Claire's confidence. *Her smile is mesmerizing,* he thought as she grabbed a clean cloth from a stack on top of a dryer.

"This doesn't help us much now—but right after the stain, you should try to dab at it with a clean towel right away. You always want to blot, not rub. Rubbing at it will only spread it like bad gossip. Club soda helps, too." She used the cloth to show James what she meant, then handed it to him.

As James tried to mimic her efforts, she jumped in, grabbing his hand to adjust his motion. "Easy, there. Don't rub. You're not trying to start a fire!" James glanced down at her hand on his, causing Claire to release it quickly.

"Wow. You're on a roll with the one-liners today," James said, his eyebrows raising and his mouth forming into a sideways smile.

"After being stuck in this laundromat for most of my life, you pick up a few things. My dad was the king of laundry jokes. I guess I learned from him." Claire shifted her weight, uncomfortable with the subject of her parents. "Okay, so, our next step, given that the stain is set, is a cold water rinse. We want to try to force the stain out the way it came in, so we work from the back of the stain."

James nodded, following Claire over to the large laundry sink in the back, acutely aware of the quick change in her demeanor. But she quickly shook it off and began illustrating the cold rinse. As the water ran through the back of the stain, Claire explained, "You want to flush it out from behind—push it back out."

"The solution to this entire situation was dabbing at it and cold water?" James stared at Claire, his eyes widening in mock surprise.

"Oh, no. No, no, no, no, you poor, clueless man." She grinned. "We are just getting started. This is a multi-step process! I'm about to show you the real magic—the holy trinity. Do you think you can handle it?"

"Yes, oh great and powerful laundry master. Show me your ways. I'm ready." James bowed deeply toward Claire, his eyes twinkling as they joked.

"Are you *sure* you're prepared for this?" Claire asked, eying him cautiously. "Once you know this trick, you will forever be banned from throwing out your shirts after run-ins with your morning caffeine... It's a big step."

"I can take it. I'm ready." James nodded.

"Okay. Here we go. The secret recipe..." Claire grabbed a small bottle of dish soap from a cabinet under the sink, then a bottle of white vinegar, placing them side by side on the wide rim of the basin. "Dish soap, vinegar, and water." She poured some vinegar into an empty spray bottle, then added a few drops of dish soap and topped it with water before shaking the bottle to mix the solution. "This works on most stains. The soap cuts the grease, the vinegar breaks down the tannins, and water keeps it all moving. It even works on wine—and wine is TOUGH."

James watched Claire, impressed. "You know, you make this whole laundry thing look... kind of badass!"

"Stain-fighting *is* badass. Do you have any idea how many wedding gowns, christening dresses, communion gowns, and... clumsy men's shirts... I've rescued over the years?"

"Saving family heirlooms and men's careers, one garment at a time!"

"I should really make that my tagline. Put it on a sign and hang it up somewhere in here." Claire sprayed the cleaning cocktail at the stain, then blotted at it with a fresh towel with practiced movements. "You want to coax it out. No scrubbing. This isn't TLC."

James looked confused.

"The TLC song? No Scrubs? Nevermind. That joke was mine. It clearly didn't land well. I'll stick to my dad's." Claire chuckled as she worked on the stain, then handed the solution and towel to James. "Your turn!"

"Are you going to hold my hand again?" James said, a flirty grin forming.

Claire blushed. "I... I... uh... I didn't mean to... um—" she searched for words but came up with none.

"I liked it," James confessed, interrupting her flustered

stuttering and reaching for her hand. "Show me," he said in more of a whisper than he'd planned. *What am I doing?!*

Claire blushed but allowed James to take her hand. She moved it to rest on his fingers, leading him in the proper dabbing motion. "Gentle. Like this," she said softly, guiding his hand across the stain.

"Then what?" James asked, a hint of wanting in his tone.

"You just have to keep at it for a while to make sure the stain—" Claire stopped mid-sentence as she felt James' free hand circle her waist, drawing her toward him.

"I'm more interested in the method than the results at this point," James teased, his voice huskier.

"I'm not sure this is about laundry anymore," she mumbled.

"It isn't." James dropped the towel onto the edge of the sink and brought his hand to Claire's face, placing two fingers beneath her chin and tilting it upward to look at him. "It may never have been," he added, moving his face closer to hers.

As James began to close the gap between them, their lips brushed softly for a mere moment before—

CRASH! A clattering noise from the office caused them to pull apart and race toward the half-door, leaving their kiss unfinished.

They found Chaos standing in the center of the office, surrounded by a cascade of buttons from the antique button jar Claire kept on her desk—the one her mother had collected over decades, filled with buttons from every garment that had ever lost one in the wash. Hundreds of buttons of every size, shape, and color were scattered across the floor like confetti. Chaos wagged his tail, clearly proud of his destruction. Walt sat at a safe distance, observing the chaos with the dignified detachment of a dog who wanted it known he'd had nothing to do with this.

"Oh no," Claire breathed, dropping to her knees. "Those were my mom's."

James was beside her immediately. "We'll find them all. Every single one." He started picking up buttons, placing them carefully in his palm. A tiny pearl button. A brass military button. A translucent pink one shaped like a flower.

Claire picked up a large wooden button and turned it over in her fingers. "This one was from my dad's favorite flannel. The shirt fell apart years ago, but Mom kept the button." Her voice was steady, but her hands weren't.

They worked in silence for several minutes, crawling across the office floor while two dogs watched—one guilty, one indifferent. James found buttons behind the desk, under the chair, wedged in the gap between the floorboards. He placed each one in the jar with the care of someone handling something precious, because he understood that they were.

"I think that's most of them," he said finally, scanning the floor.

"Most," Claire agreed. She looked at the jar, now two-thirds full where it had been overflowing. Some buttons had probably rolled under the machines, into cracks, under cabinets. Lost, like the garments they'd come from. Like the people who'd worn them.

"I'll come back with a flashlight," James said. "We'll find the rest."

Claire looked at him—this man in an expensive sweater, on his hands and knees on the floor of a laundromat office, holding a handful of buttons like they were diamonds—

and felt something shift in her chest. Something she wasn't ready to name.

"Thank you," she said softly.

"Don't thank me. Thank Chaos." He shot a look at his puppy. "Actually, don't thank Chaos. He's grounded."

Chaos, hearing his name, wagged his tail harder and stepped directly onto a button, which skittered across the floor. Walt sighed.

"I should probably head out," James said, standing and brushing off his knees. "Before my dog destroys any more family heirlooms."

"Probably wise." Claire stood too, clutching the button jar against her chest. "Same time tomorrow?"

"Wouldn't miss it." He paused at the half-door. "For what it's worth, I think your mom had great taste in buttons."

Claire smiled. "She had great taste in everything. Except curtains. Her curtains were objectively terrible."

James laughed—a real, surprised laugh that echoed through the laundromat—and something in Claire's chest tightened again. She was going to have to deal with that eventually.

But not today.

Chaos

CLAIRE

Chapter 10

AFTER JAMES LEFT, CLAIRE SAT AT HER DESK WITH the button jar in her lap, running her thumb over the rim. Some buttons were still missing—rolled under machines or wedged into floorboards, lost to the same entropy that claimed socks and earring backs and people you loved. She'd find them eventually. Or she wouldn't. Either way, the jar was lighter than it had been that morning, and the absence felt disproportionate to its size.

She set the jar back on the desk, anchoring it further

from the edge this time, and turned her attention to the day's remaining work. There were wash-and-fold orders to finish, and Carla was arriving any minute to cover the laundromat while Claire headed to her Yappy Hour planning meeting.

As she waited, Claire's mind kept circling back to the moment on the office floor—James on his knees, placing buttons into the jar with the care of someone handling relics. The way he'd said, *"We'll find the rest."* As if it were a given. As if he'd already decided that her losses were his to help recover.

Don't read into it, she told herself. *He's a nice man who helped pick up buttons. That's all. People do nice things. It doesn't mean anything.*

Except it did. She knew it did. And that was the terrifying part.

She shook her head and pulled herself back to the present. There was work to do. There was always work to do. She'd text James later about scheduling another laundry lesson—he'd mentioned wanting to learn how to separate colors, which meant he was either genuinely hopeless or looking for an excuse to come back. She suspected both.

Claire had also planned to text Dr. Dennis after the Yappy Hour meeting for a walk in the park, but after the events of the day, she wasn't sure if that was even still appropriate. *Is he still going to be interested? Am I interested?*

She hadn't dated anyone in what felt like ages, let alone entertained the idea of dating two men at once. She knew that's what dating in the early stages technically *was* nowadays. Still, somehow, the idea of getting to know more than one person at a time in a romantic sense seemed overwhelming to her—and downright impossible with her schedule. Then again, she hadn't exactly had the opportunity. Online dating was a no-go for her. She had heard enough horror stories to stay away from the dating apps, and it was nearly impossible to find anyone to date otherwise, except, apparently, this week.

Before she could spiral any further, the door flung open, and Carla sauntered in. "Claire!" she called. "No need to fear! Your Carla is here. I brought Matt along to keep me company... Laundry is boring."

Matt walked in behind his wife, chuckling. "How would you know?" he muttered, just loudly enough for her to hear.

"I do laundry!" Carla pouted. "I mean, sometimes. Occasionally. You always get to it first!"

"Because I got tired of you attempting to create a life-size model of laundry Mount Everest," Matt snickered.

Carla folded her arms across her chest. "Whatever," she said, ending the conversation without having to admit her husband was right.

"In here," Claire called out from the office.

Carla's jaw dropped as she caught sight of the button jar, still not quite full, and the faint evidence of the floor-crawling cleanup mission. She elbowed her husband in the ribs. "What happened in here?"

"Long story. Chaos knocked over the button jar. James helped me pick them all up." She paused. "On his hands and knees. Like they were diamonds."

Carla's eyes widened. "*James* was here? Crawling around on the floor picking up buttons? That's the most romantic thing I've ever heard."

"It wasn't romantic. It was practical. There were buttons everywhere."

"Claire. A man in expensive clothes got on the floor to

pick up your dead mother's buttons. That is the *definition* of romantic."

Claire didn't have a rebuttal for that. She changed the subject. "Anyway, he left already. We're doing another laundry lesson next week."

Matt glanced at Carla. "Any chance Carla could get some laundry lessons?"

Carla spun slightly on her heel and gave Matt a playful punch in the shoulder. "Shush. I do laundry just fine. And if you don't shush about it, I'll be sure *not* to wash that thing you like me to wear..."

Claire put her hands over her ears. "I don't need to hear this, guys—and I have to leave, anyway. There's a list of *FAQ*s on the desk in the office in case any customers come in and ask you about anything—but most people are regulars and already know the drill."

As she spoke, Claire clipped the leash onto Walter's collar. "I don't expect to be very long, but feel free to text me if anything comes up that you aren't sure about."

"We got this. As Matt so clearly expressed before, he's the laundry *master*." Carla squeezed Matt's behind playfully as she spoke.

Claire looked at the two of them, shook her head, laughing. "You two never change, and I love it."

"And I love you," Carla said, blowing a kiss to Claire. "Now, get out of here! We'll be fine. We won't burn down your laundromat!"

Matt shifted his gaze to his wife, raising his eyebrows. "Why? Why would you even say that?!" he asked incredulously.

"I dunno. Seemed funny at the time," she said, chuckling.

"It wasn't!" both Claire and Matt stated in unison.

Claire rolled her eyes at her friend, grinned, and walked out the door holding Walter's leash in her hand and ushering him forward. "Call me if you need anything," she shouted over her shoulder.

Lavender and Lye

CLAIRE

Chapter 11

IT STARTED WITH A SUPPLY ORDER.

Claire was restocking the detergent cabinet—a task she did every Tuesday with the mechanical efficiency of someone who'd done it roughly five hundred times—when a box on the top shelf shifted and something fluttered to the floor. A folded piece of paper, yellowed at the edges, the creases so deep they'd become permanent.

She picked it up and unfolded it, and her mother's handwriting stared back at her.

Mom's Miracle Mix — For the Stains That Won't Quit

The letters were round and careful, written in the purple ink her mother had used for everything—grocery lists, birthday cards, the labels on the holiday cookie tins. Below the title was a recipe, laid out with the precision of someone who took chemistry personally:

2 cups washing soda (NOT baking soda, Claire, they're different!) 1 cup borax 1 bar castile soap, grated fine 15 drops lavender oil (the good kind, not the dollar store stuff) Mix dry. Store in the blue jar. Use 2 tablespoons per load. Works on everything except regret and red wine. For red wine, call me.

Claire read the last line three times. Then she sat down on an upturned bucket and pressed the paper against her chest.

She didn't cry. Not right away. The grief arrived the way it always did—not as a wave but as a slow leak, seeping through cracks she thought she'd sealed. Her mother had written this for her. Not for a customer, not for a manual, but for *her*—a cheat sheet for the day Claire would be standing in this exact spot, alone, needing to know what to do.

You knew, Claire thought. *You knew I'd be here without you, and you left me instructions.*

She sat there for a while, breathing in the familiar smell of the laundromat—industrial soap, warm cotton, the faintest trace of lavender from the dryer sheets she bought in bulk. Her mother's smell. The smell of every childhood memory that mattered.

Eventually, she stood up, smoothed the paper flat, and carried it to the office. She placed it on the desk and stared at it. Then, because she was her mother's daughter and her mother would have turned grief into action, she pulled out the supplies.

She had washing soda. She had borax. She had castile soap—a bar of it, untouched, that she'd been using as a doorstop for the supply closet because it was the exact right weight. She even had lavender oil, though she suspected it was the dollar store kind her mother had specifically warned against.

She grated the soap by hand, the way the recipe instructed. The repetitive motion was soothing—back and forth against the grater, the soap curling into delicate shavings that piled up on the cutting board like snow. Her mother used to do this at the kitchen table while listening to the radio, singing along to Motown with the unselfconscious joy of a woman who knew she couldn't carry a tune and didn't care.

Claire measured the washing soda and borax, mixed the dry ingredients in a large bowl, added the soap shavings, and counted out fifteen drops of lavender oil. The scent hit her immediately—sharp and sweet and so achingly familiar that it bypassed her brain entirely and went straight to the place in her chest where she kept the things she couldn't talk about.

She stirred the mixture with a wooden spoon, watching the ingredients combine into a fine, fragrant powder. It looked right. It smelled right. She scooped two tablespoons into a warm load of whites she'd been running and watched the machine fill.

Twenty-eight minutes later, she pulled the clothes out.

They were fine. Clean, soft, adequately brightened. But they weren't the same. The miracle her mother had promised—the impossible, intangible quality that had made her mother's laundry better than anyone else's, the reason customers drove past three other laundromats to come to this one—wasn't in the recipe. It had never been in the recipe.

It had been in her mother's hands. In the way she touched the fabric, checked the temperature, knew by instinct whether a stain needed more time or a gentler touch. It was in the hum she carried while she worked, the warmth she brought to the room, the love she folded into every garment as if each one contained a person she cared about.

Claire couldn't replicate that. No recipe could.

She sat back down on the bucket, held the paper in both hands, and cried. Not the polite, containable kind—the ugly, gulping, mascara-destroying kind that made Walt emerge from the office with alarm in his eyes and press his body against her legs. She cried for her mother's handwriting. For the purple ink. For the fact that she would never be able to call about red wine. For the empty space in the laundromat where a woman used to dance between the machines, and for the daughter who was trying, every single day, to fill it.

When she was done, she washed her face in the laundry sink, dried it with a clean towel from the stack, and folded the recipe carefully. She didn't put it back in the cabinet. Instead, she slipped it into the frame of her parents' photo on the office shelf, tucked behind the picture where only she would know it was there.

Then she went back to restocking the detergent cabinet. There were twelve bottles left to shelve, and a wash-and-fold order due by five, and a dog who needed dinner, and a life that required her to keep going.

She kept going. She always did.

But that night, after closing, she added lavender oil to the mop water—the good kind, ordered online, express shipping—and cleaned the floors the way her mother used to. And when the laundromat smelled right again, she locked the door, went upstairs, and slept better than she had in weeks.

The Crush

~~~

JAMES

Chapter 12

JAMES SAT IN HIS CAR WAITING ON A RED LIGHT. Out of the corner of his eye, he glanced a woman walking toward the park across the street with a large, dark-colored dog. *Could that be... ? Was that...?* He squinted his eyes, trying to get a better look despite the sun shining in his eyes. No—it wasn't Claire (or Walter for that matter).

For the love of God, man! What are you doing to yourself?! He groaned and rested his head in his hands. Three quick beeps from the car behind him snapped him to attention. Chaos let out a quick bark in response to the noise. "I'm going, I'm going. Relax!" he muttered, shifting his car into gear and stepping on the gas.

James couldn't believe how transfixed he was with this Claire woman after only a couple of meetings. It's not as if he hadn't had opportunities to be with plenty of women over the years—gorgeous, successful, and powerful women! He'd just never felt the timing was right, and the whole no-strings-attached thing got old pretty quickly. It wasn't his vibe. In fact, until then, his *vibe* hadn't really existed for years. His career always came first. He didn't have time for women or relationships.

As he tried to focus on the road ahead of him, his phone rang through the car's Bluetooth system. He glanced at the number that appeared on the car's screen and winced. *T.M. Enterprises.* He'd managed to avoid giving them a final answer about the job and relocation by dodging several phone calls from Bridget, Mr. Marzini's assistant. He felt conflicted and couldn't even figure out why. This should be an easy decision. It was what he'd worked his entire life for, the opportunity to reach the top!

Somehow, though, the prospect of giving the final 'yes' to *T.M. Enterprises* gave him an unanticipated sense of fear and dread. He had never been afraid of change before, and he couldn't quite assign a particular reason for it this time —but, somehow, all of a sudden, he didn't want to leave. He refused to even consider that all this uncertainty was over a woman. No, it had to be something else. He just had to figure it out.

He smiled, reaching over to give Chaos a quick pet. "What are we going to do with me, Chaos? I'm a mess."

When James reached his home, he began to feel nostalgic again. *What is wrong with me?* He shook it off and climbed the steps to his home office, turning on his computer to check some emails and get some work done. As he clicked into his inbox, he saw an email from Bridget at *T.M.* requesting that he return her call by the next day to go over the details of his relocation. He noticed that she made it seem as if the option to say no didn't exist. And he would be crazy to turn down the offer. It would be life-changing— but maybe that was the problem.

He scrolled through several other emails, mostly junk or information he was already aware of. He had other work to do, but his focus was elsewhere. His thoughts kept wandering until he found himself perusing the website of a certain laundromat and dog wash...

The website was, to put it charitably, a relic. It had the look of something built on a free template sometime during the Obama administration and never updated. The photos were slightly blurry, the color scheme was aggressive teal and orange, and the "Hours" page still listed holiday hours for 2021. There was a visitor counter at the bottom that read "You are visitor #4,312," which, given the site's age, suggested roughly three visitors per day.

And yet, it had charm. The way Claire's personality bled through the clunky design reminded him of the laundromat itself—not polished, not optimized, but unmistakably *her*. The home page featured Walter as the face of the business, photographed mid-yawn in a way that made him look like he was roaring. The tagline read: "Where your laundry gets a second chance (and your dog gets a bath)."

I could fix this site in a weekend, James thought, then caught himself. *Since when do you redesign websites for women you've known for three days? That's not normal behavior. Stop it.*

He reached the *About Us* section, gazing at the owner's headshot—Claire. She was smiling in the photo, but it wasn't her real smile—the one that crinkled the corners of her eyes and made her look like she was about to say something sarcastic. This was the polite, camera-ready version. He preferred the other one. His eyes scanned the screen, reading her bio:

Hi there! I'm Claire, owner and operator of *Dirty Laundry/Bubbles & Barks,* your neighborhood laundromat and dog wash. We've been serving the laundry needs of the community for generations. As somewhat of a laundry miracle worker, I'm here to help tackle your impossible stains.

I took over the family business after my parents passed away, and while it's been challenging running the place solo, I couldn't imagine doing anything else, but I do have my own style! So, you may notice some changes around here... What started as a traditional laundromat has evolved into something special—a unique opportunity where you and your four-legged family members can come to get your coats (and other apparel) squeaky clean. There's something magical about watching dogs and their humans connect over the universal experience of laundry day!

My business partner and resident troublemaker is Sir Walter the Bouvier. At almost five years old, Walt keeps me (and my clientele) on our toes with his creative interpretations of "helping out" around the shop. Whether he is transforming my own clean laundry into his personal bedding or finding something equally inconvenient to get into, there's never a dull moment around here.

In addition to my interest in dirty laundry, I am deeply passionate about bringing the community together. I'm working to bring some exciting events to fruition, including a monthly *Yappy Hour* dog meet-and-greet at the park across the street. Stay tuned for information about our first session this month!

Stop by anytime. Walt and I are always happy to help you tackle all of your laundry challenges—and we love meeting new furry friends. Just don't be surprised if you leave with a few extra dog hairs on your clothes... it's all part of the charm!

He couldn't believe it, but James was pretty sure he had his first real crush in many years. With the worst possible timing. He closed out of the website, rolling his eyes and picking up his phone to call Bridget back.

Get yourself together, James.

The phone rang twice on the other end of the line before a female voice picked up. "It's about time!" Bridget answered the phone.

"Is that normally how you answer the company phone line?" James asked, chuckling.

"Caller ID," Bridget replied. "Mr. Marzini isn't used to being kept waiting when it comes to filling company positions. It makes him grumpy, and I've had to deal with the brunt of it. So, what's the deal, Mr. Dorland? When can you make Silicon Valley your new home?"

"I... I just need a little time to sort out a few personal things on my end."

"But you *do* want the position?"

"I... yes, of course."

"Can you be ready in one month? We will handle your housing arrangements. I'll send several different options for you to review by email. Let me know which you prefer, and I'll get it all set up."

"One month? That's really soon, isn't it?" James winced.

"Not when Mr. Marzini is involved. He doesn't like to leave things up in the air," Bridget explained. "It makes him uncomfortable."

Speaking of uncomfortable... Things were moving quickly, but he should have anticipated that. Business is business.

"Okay. One month it is," James confirmed, trying to sound more sure of himself than he felt. *This is what you've always wanted, man. What is the matter with you? Snap out of it.*

"Fabulous. I'll let Mr. Marzini know, and I'll have the available housing options sent for your review by this afternoon. Try to let me know which you prefer as soon as possible. They're all really nice, honestly. We have other new hires to house, but Mr. Marzini is giving you first choice... but, he doesn't like to wait around. With that said, Congratulations, Mr. Dorland—and welcome to *T.M. Enterprises.* Mr. Marzini has high hopes for you in the company. I'm sure he'll want to welcome you on board personally in the coming days. I'll reach out to arrange a call."

"Sounds good," James said. "And, thank you!" Again, he tried to sound enthusiastic, but somewhere in the pit of his stomach was a small but growing sense of dread, a feeling that he was about to make a mistake. *It's just anxiety,* he told himself, reaching down to scoop Chaos into his lap.

"We'll be happy wherever we are, right, little buddy?" he asked his dog, leaning down to snuggle his face against the small ball of fur. Chaos looked up at him and licked him across the cheek. "I just hope the housing options are dog-friendly, or we will have an entirely different problem on our hands."

The Park

Chapter 13

WALT PRACTICALLY DRAGGED CLAIRE IN through the park entrance, where she was meeting up with the town's recreation director to confirm some of the final event details. The Rec department was in charge of all of the activities held within the park and would be assisting with getting the first event off the ground.

Claire hoped that after the first few months of *Yappy Hour*, it would be relatively simple to plan—but this time was taking a significant amount of work because it was the kickoff. There would be raffles, giveaways, food trucks, and several dog-themed vendors participating in the first session. All of the proceeds would go toward the dog park fund!

Claire sat on a bench near the center of the park beside the fountain that had been there for as long as she could remember. She had fond memories of tossing coins over her shoulder into the water alongside her parents, making wish after wish. She wondered why so many of those wishes went unfulfilled, especially those she continued to make well into her adult life. Coins hadn't saved either of her parents, nor had they brought her the love of her life. *I guess I'll just keep wishing, right, Walt? Eventually, something will pan out!*

Walt began to jump in place excitedly, eyeing a tall, thin woman who was making her way over to Claire and Walter. "Hello there, Mr. Walter. Hi, Claire," the woman said, grinning at them both and leaning in for a hug.

"Hi, Tina," Claire replied, hugging the woman she'd also known since childhood. Tina was somewhat older, but she had been coming into the laundromat for years. They had developed a repertoire over the years—and they worked well together. She lived in the apartment complex just down the street, and her parents had been somewhat close friends with Claire's. Both were passionate about keeping a tight-knit local community.

"So excited to get *Yappy Hour* off the ground. We've got most of the logistics nailed down on our end, and everything is moving along." Tina reached down and began to pet Walter, bending down to get closer and give him a proper greeting.

"Amazing," Claire said, smiling. "I've been spreading the word through the shop, fliers, some social media advertising, and so on. People seem really excited!"

For several minutes, the women discussed the event plans, advertising, vendor placement, and potential fundraising ideas before moving on to discuss the steps necessary to create the dog park. It was a productive conversation, and Claire felt confident that her dream would soon become a reality. She only hoped it would boost business at the dog wash—and maybe even bring in some new laundromat customers once they started coming in with their pups. *Who wouldn't want to bring their best friend with them to do laundry?*

Claire knew she was part of a very small minority of people who actually enjoyed doing laundry. It sounded strange, but to her, it represented second chances—even though she was still waiting for her happily ever after. She could take the worst stain, the most epic mess, and make it look brand new with just a little know-how and elbow grease. *If only I could do that in my own life!* She gazed heavenward as her thoughts wandered.

Finally, they wrapped up their meeting and set up a call for a few days later to go over the few outstanding follow-up items in connection with *Yappy Hour*. After Tina said her goodbyes to Claire and Walter and made her way back toward the Rec office, Claire pulled out her phone and saw that she had missed a call. *Dr. Dennis.*

He didn't leave a voicemail, but had sent a follow-up text:

Dennis: Hey! Are we still on for the park?

Claire pondered a moment before she began her reply. What was the harm in seeing him today as planned—even with James occupying a large portion of her mind? She barely knew him! Anyway, time and time again, she'd been advised to date around and see what was out there. And she wasn't officially *dating* anyone, even casually! She was just... seeing what happened.

She couldn't help but laugh at herself. "I sound like the

guys I used to date back when I tried online dating..." She scoffed. 'Let's see what happens' seemed to be the overwhelming response to 'What are you looking for?' No one wanted to openly admit they weren't actually looking for a relationship, at least an exclusive one. It was one of the reasons she'd lost interest in the whole dating scene. She'd rather be alone!

Claire: Sure! I'm here with Walter now. Carla is watching the laundromat. No catastrophes over there as far as I know... yet. Matt's with her, so that helps!

Dennis: Awesome! I have a gap in patients right after I finish up with this cat. It licked a scented candle, enjoyed it, proceeded to eat more, then threw up the glittery purple wax all over his owner's bed.

Claire: Oh my God! Is it okay?

Dennis: The owner wasn't sure how much he consumed. I Googled to find out the candle ingredients. Now, I just have to check him out. As far as I can tell from my initial assessment, it appears the cat has no regrets—and that he will be just fine. They don't teach this in vet school.

Claire snorted. *Okay, fine. He's funny. It wouldn't hurt to see how this goes.*

Claire: Walter and I will be by the fountain whenever you can get here. I'm in no rush, so just stop over as soon as you know glitter kitty is okay!

Dennis: Glitter Kitty sounds like a stripper name. See you in a few!

"Come on, Walt. Let's take a little stroll while we wait," Claire told her dog, who leapt to his feet, clearly ready to explore. This was why she wanted a dog park so badly. It would be so nice to have a place to let him run off-leash without worrying. A place where he could enjoy the company of other friendly dogs.

Walt led the way, taking Claire on several nearby paths. Whenever he tried to pull her away from view of the fountain, she urged him back gently. She wanted to be able to see Dr. Den—just Dennis—when he arrived.

A short while later, a man appeared in the distance. As he walked toward the fountain, Claire kept her gaze fixed on him. He really *was* cute. He had broad shoulders, and in his short-sleeved scrubs, his arms looked strong enough to hold even the largest, most unruly pet in place as needed... without looking like a gym rat. His stride was confident, with long steps and a sexy sway at the hip. She wasn't sure how, after all these years, she'd never really noticed it before. *Has he been working out or something?*

As Dennis noticed her and Walt walking in his direction, he smiled and waved. Claire waved back, speeding up in response to Walter's tugging.

"Hey there," Dennis said, leaning into an awkward hug with Claire, then bending to greet Walt, who lifted his front paws off the ground, placing them on his shoulders in some sort of bear hug—uh, dog hug.

"Walter! Down! Ugh, I'm sorry. He has absolutely no manners." Claire pulled back gently on Walt's leash.

"You're talking to a veterinarian, remember? This is nothing I haven't dealt with before," he replied, hugging Walt back as Claire loosened the slack on the leash again. "You won't believe this, but most of my patients do *not* get excited to see me. I take this as the best type of compliment!"

Claire laughed. "Well, that's good to hear. Maybe someday we'll do some training with him or something. Although, I think that ship has already sailed. He's pretty set in his ways..."

"If giving free hugs—and cleaning your office floor with

detergent—are his worst offenses, I don't think you need to worry about teaching the old dog new tricks."

"As his personal physician, you know very well those make up only a very small selection of his crimes... Still, I guess he could be worse." Claire glanced down at Walter, who had released Dennis from his paw-hold and was now sitting, attempting to give his paw to the vet over and over, in a fruitless attempt to get the treats that were typically kept in his pockets during vet visits.

"Sorry, pup. I left them in the office. My last patient was a cat. I wasn't thinking!" Dennis raised his arms and shrugged in an apologetic gesture, and Walter gave up and began sniffing around the area.

"Speaking of which, how is glitter kitty?" Claire raised her eyebrows in question, a smile teasing her lips.

"Ahh, well... glitter kitty will never consume another candle again."

Claire's jaw dropped. "Oh, no! Is he...?"

"Oh! Oh, no! He's fine. He didn't die or anything. Jeez! I just meant that I think he probably learned his lesson." Dennis slapped his hand against his forehead in a face palm.

"Not if he's anything like Walter. He never learns." Claire gave her dog a look.

"That's true. He does have a laundry list of offenses in his record. Pun intended."

Claire grinned at Dennis. "Smooth," she joked.

"Well, what can I say? I haven't really spent much time with women since my divorce. I'm still learning."

"No, it's okay. The puns are good. I'm just teasing. So, how have things been? You know, since the divorce?"

"I don't know. Okay. I have been spending more time working and just trying to stay busy. Otherwise, I get sort of lonely, I guess. It's weird not to go home to someone after so many years, but it was the right decision. We had grown apart. We had known for a while that we were forcing things. The truth of it is that my ex-wife and I were always better friends than a couple." Dennis chuckled. "It just took us a long time to figure it out. We are still on good terms. It was relatively amicable, but even so, it hasn't exactly been easy to get used to some of the changes."

Claire nodded. "I think that's one of my biggest fears."

"What is?"

"Well, I've been on my own so long that I'm scared of settling for the wrong person just to have someone. What's worse? Being alone or being with someone who, after all is said and done, isn't right for you?"

Dennis reached over and squeezed Claire's shoulder. "I didn't expect this to get so deep, but since we're already on the topic... I think when it's right, you'll just know. I'll share a secret with you." He winked at Claire. "You ready?"

"Sure," Claire said. "Bring it on."

"You asked for it. Now, don't think I'm a terrible person, but I knew my ex wasn't meant to be my forever person pretty early on in our relationship. Honestly, I think she knew deep down, too. We were young and we enjoyed each other's company. We learned a lot from each other and had a lot of fun doing it." Dennis shrugged. "But somehow, we stayed together long past the fun parts. Then, before we even knew what was happening, we got lost in the shuffle of all the things we were *supposed* to be doing. Our friends were all getting married. Our parents were looking forward to a beautiful wedding. They thought it was time for grand-kids, and so on. So, we got swept out to sea in all the things couples at our age were *expected* to do."

He ran a hand through his hair, then continued. "We did the whole expensive wedding, buy a house thing—but we weren't really happy. Not the way you're supposed to be when you find the right person. It was a façade, even though neither of us would admit it at the time. I think... I think once we realized that children weren't in the cards for us, it became a lot easier to part ways."

"If you're trying to calm my fears about being with the wrong person, you're epically failing right now..." Claire chuckled, but her face showed concern.

"You're missing my point. The point is, you'll know if it's right or wrong. Probably pretty early on. You just have to listen to yourself—and not anyone else."

Dennis smiled at Claire. He was being so open and honest, vulnerable even. For a moment, she felt herself wishing she felt a spark or even a hint of chemistry, but it just wasn't there. Even when he touched her, it was like the comforting hand of a sibling or a best friend. When James touched her, it sent chills down her spine. *On the other hand, maybe that was a damn warning from my nervous system to stay away...*

"Anyway, I guess what I'm trying to get at here," Dennis began, "is that I can tell you're not into me in the way I'd hoped. So, I want to say here and now that it's perfectly okay! Honestly, I feel more of a friend vibe between us, too. So, let's roll with it. I could use a female friend to point me in the right direction as I navigate the strange new world of dating in my old age. Things sure have changed."

He opened his phone and gestured to a folder on his home screen titled "Dating Apps: UGH!"

An overwhelming sense of relief fell over Claire, and she laughed. A friend. She could always use another friend, and who knows, maybe someday she'd develop deeper feelings. Stranger things had happened. But, for the time being, it removed the pressure she'd been feeling. It made things less awkward. She hated to admit it, but it also gave her less of a sense of guilt over her rapidly developing (and confusing) feelings she had for James.

"I could definitely use a friend," Claire admitted. "Most of mine are all wrapped up in their families, work, and so on. At least you know we'll see each other often, even if just for vet visits!" She glanced at Walter, who was licking something of unknown origin off a park bench. "Speaking of which, does this friendship come with complimentary veterinary consultations?" She grinned, gesturing to her dog.

"Absolutely. Call anytime. Consider me your personal doggy disaster hotline. You've poured enough money into my little practice over the years with his shenanigans." Dennis laughed and bent down to pet Walter as Claire pulled him away from the bench, the current object of his affection.

Together, the three walked a few loops around the park, pausing to enjoy garden views and to take in the antics of several squirrels, a few other dogs, and a family of ducks. They talked about their lives, but Claire didn't bring up James. Neither did Dennis. She wondered if he was curious about the earlier meetup he had crashed. *Maybe he sensed I had feelings for James, and that's where the friendship decision came from,* Claire pondered, wondering if there was a chance he was choosing friendship from the jump to avoid the potential heartache of not being "picked."

Either way, Claire felt relieved.

Dennis's phone alarm began ringing, indicating he had to head back for his next patient. So, they parted as friends, with Claire returning to the laundromat and Dennis heading back to his veterinary practice.

As he turned to leave, Dennis paused. "Hey, Claire?

That guy from the laundromat—James. The one with the puppy. Does he have a vet yet?"

Claire blinked. "I... don't think so, actually. Chaos is pretty new."

"Would you mind passing along my number? Or giving me his? New puppy owners always need a good vet, and I could use the business." He said it casually, like it was nothing. Like a vet drumming up clients.

Claire didn't entirely buy the explanation, but she couldn't pinpoint why. "Sure," she said, pulling out her phone and texting Dennis James's number. "There you go. His name in my phone is James Shirt, but his real name is James Dorland. Long story."

"Always is with you." Dennis grinned, pocketed his phone, and headed back toward the office. Claire watched him go, feeling like she'd just handed over something she didn't fully understand yet.

Off the Leash

JAMES

Chapter 14

THE TEXT FROM DENNIS ARRIVED ON A TUESDAY evening, casual enough to seem spontaneous: *Hey, want to grab a beer? There's a place on Elm that doesn't card dogs. I checked.*

James almost declined. He had emails to answer, a presentation to finalize, and a housing preference form from T.M. Enterprises that he'd been avoiding for the better part of a week. But something about the invitation felt deliberate in a way that made him curious, so he texted back: *Sure. 7 work?*

The bar was called *The Tap Room*, and it lived up to its name by having taps and being a room. It was the kind of place where the bartender knew everyone's name and the peanut shells on the floor were considered ambiance. Dennis was already there when James arrived, sitting at a corner booth with a golden retriever mix at his feet who appeared to be asleep and possibly drunk.

"That's Biscuit," Dennis said, nodding at the dog. "She's a regular. Belongs to the bartender. She's not actually drunk, she's just like that."

James sat down and ordered a local IPA. Dennis was drinking something amber and unhurried. Chaos, tucked under James's arm, immediately squirmed free and toddled over to investigate Biscuit, who opened one eye, assessed the puppy, and closed it again. Chaos took this as an invitation to curl up beside her.

"So," James said. "What's the occasion?"

Dennis took a sip of his beer. "No occasion. I just figured we should get to know each other, since we're apparently orbiting the same person."

The directness caught James off guard. He'd expected small talk first—sports, weather, the universal male bonding ritual of pretending not to have emotions for the first twenty minutes of any social encounter. Instead, Dennis had walked straight to the point with the efficiency of a man who spent his days extracting porcupine quills from nervous animals.

"Claire," James said.

"Claire," Dennis confirmed. He leaned back in the booth. "Listen, I'm not going to do the thing where I threaten you or tell you I'll break your legs if you hurt her. That's performative, and honestly, I'd throw my back out. I'm a vet, not a bouncer."

James laughed. "Appreciated."

"But I want to tell you something about her that she won't tell you herself, because she's pathologically incapable of asking for sympathy." Dennis set his glass down and turned it slowly on the coaster. "I've known Claire since we were kids. Same school, same town, same everything. Her parents ran that laundromat for thirty years. Her mom was the kind of person who made everyone feel like family. Her dad could fix anything with duct tape and stubbornness. They were good people. The best, actually."

"She's told me a little about them."

"Then she's told you more than she tells most people." Dennis looked at him steadily. "When her mom got sick, Claire was twenty-three. She'd just gotten a job at a marketing firm in the city—first person in her family to get a college degree, first to get a corporate job. She was good at it, too. But she came home. Didn't hesitate. Quit the job, moved back, took over the laundromat so her dad could focus on her mom."

James was quiet.

"Her mom passed eight months later. Her dad... he tried. But he'd been with her mom since they were seventeen. He didn't know how to exist without her. He died the following spring. Heart attack, officially. But everyone in town knows he just stopped wanting to wake up."

The bar noise continued around them—pool balls clacking, someone laughing too loud, a country song playing from speakers that had survived since the nineties. James stared at his beer.

"She was twenty-four," Dennis continued. "Twenty-four years old, running a failing laundromat by herself, grieving both parents, trying to figure out how to fix machines she'd never been trained on and manage a business she'd never wanted. The town helped where it could. I started doing free wellness checks on Walt. Carla and Matt brought her groceries. Gia and Ben fed her. But mostly, she just... did it. Every day. Open the doors, run the machines, fold the clothes, close the doors. Over and over. For three years."

"Why are you telling me this?" James asked, though he already knew.

Dennis met his eyes. "Because she let you in. And I don't think you understand how rare that is. Claire doesn't let people in. She lets people *near*—she'll joke with them, help them, feed their dogs, organize community events. But *in?* Past the walls? Into the part of her that's still that twenty-four-year-old kid trying to hold it all together?" He shook his head. "I've known her for twenty years and I'm still on the outside of that wall. You walked through it in a week."

James opened his mouth, then closed it.

"I'm not telling you what to do," Dennis said. "I'm not her dad, and she'd kill me if she knew I was having this conversation. But she deserves someone who knows the weight of what she's carrying. Not just the charming parts. Not just the laundry jokes and the dog chaos and the flip-flops. The real stuff. The three a.m. stuff. The 'I can't afford to fix the dryer but I'll figure it out' stuff."

"I know," James said quietly.

"Do you?" Dennis asked. Not accusatory. Genuinely asking.

James thought about the housing forms on his desk. The one-month timeline. The VP title. The California mansion that could swallow Claire's apartment building whole. He thought about all of it, and he felt the knot in his stomach tighten.

"I'm trying to," he said.

Dennis studied him for a long moment, then nodded slowly. "That's an honest answer. Probably the right one, too." He picked up his beer. "Now, tell me about this puppy of yours. Chaos? What kind of name is Chaos for a dog?"

"Have you met him?"

"Fair point." Dennis grinned, and the tension broke like a rubber band snapping. They spent the next hour talking about dogs and baseball and the specific madness of small-town life, and James laughed more than he had in months. But underneath the laughter, Dennis's words sat in his chest like a stone, heavy and undeniable.

She deserves someone who knows the weight of what she's carrying.

He drove home that night and sat in his car for ten minutes before going inside. The housing forms were still on his desk. He didn't look at them. Instead, he picked up his phone and texted Claire: *How was your day?*

She responded immediately: *Walt ate a dryer sheet. So, normal. Yours?*

He smiled, typed *Better now,* and meant it more than he'd meant anything in a long time.

It's a Date

~

JAMES

Chapter 15

IT'D BE FANTASTIC IF I COULD STOP THINKING *about this woman and just work.* James pulled out his phone and dialed Claire's cell number. *Maybe I can focus if I just ask her out on a real date....*

After a couple of rings, Claire picked up. She sounded winded.

"Hello?" she answered.

"Hi, Claire. It's James."

"Yeah... Caller ID. Hey!"

James slapped his hand against his face. *Idiot.*

"Right. Of course. I, well, I wanted to see if you might want to meet tonight somewhere away from the laundromat—and away from our crazy dogs. Maybe for dinner?" There was a pause. "I mean, only if you want to," James added nervously.

"No, I mean yes. Yes, I do. I would love that." Claire caught her breath. "Dinner sounds amazing."

"Do you want to try *Charmed to Table*? Ben's been trying to get me to stop in there for a long time now. I've just been too busy, I guess."

Claire laughed. "Actually, Gia and Ben have been trying to get me in there, too, ever since they started making such big changes. So, sure! Two birds, one stone!"

"Ahh, I see how it is. Using me for a chance to cross something off your never-ending to-do list!" James joked.

"You're the one who said Ben wanted you to come in," Claire laughed. "I just agreed to accompany you."

"Fine. Fair enough. *Charmed to Table* it is. Do you want me to pick you up? I know we just met. If you want to meet there, that's fine too. Whatever you prefer." James was trying to keep his cool. He had never struggled to talk to a woman before, but with Claire, he felt like his words evaporated in mid-air just as they were leaving his lips.

"I actually have to be at the laundromat until early evening. Can you just pick me up there?"

"Sure, that works. It's on the way to the restaurant for me, too."

"Perfect," Claire said. "I can leave after seven."

"Seven, it is. I'll see you then."

"See you then."

James clicked the 'end call' button and fell backward into his chair, sucking in a giant breath. "So much for concentrating. Now I'm going to be an anxious mess the entire rest of the day," he mumbled, unable to keep a smile from escaping the corners of his mouth as he reopened several of the tabs on his computer screen one after the next, forcing himself to concentrate on the task at hand.

Somehow, he managed to finish several emails and draft a few documents he'd been procrastinating. He was moving steadily along, completing several outstanding projects, until he took a break to check his email. There, waiting in his inbox, was an email from Bridget with the subject line "URGENT – California Staff Housing Options."

Instead of joy, which such a message should have brought—a fancy promotion, dramatically higher income, and free housing—he felt nothing but dread. *Why am I even going out with Claire if I know I am going to be leaving?* He sighed and opened the email.

Dear Mr. Dorland,

Please see the attached document highlighting the housing options we can offer you. Please note that these spaces are provided by *T.M. Enterprises* as a benefit conditional on your employment with the company. Upon choosing your preference, please return the form along with the additional materials listed on the attachment. We will need this—and the employment documents you received earlier this week—completed before we can confirm your housing in one of our company-owned homes.

Please don't hesitate to reach out if you have any questions or need additional information.

Regards,

Bridget Hurley

Executive Assistant

James sighed as he clicked open the .pdf from the bottom of the email. "Holy shit," he said, his jaw dropping and eyes wide. "They're mansions! These are all... they're all mansions!"

He scrolled down the document, seeing one house larger and more luxurious than the next. Several homes were smaller but featured stunning views of the surrounding hills and mountains. One even offered a glimpse of the San Francisco Bay. Some were further from *T.M. Enterprises* headquarters than others, with the estimated commute times listed below the primary photos.

How was he supposed to decide between homes like this? Each one was more impressive than the next, but he'd never been into material things. More house meant more to maintain, and he had a feeling his free time would be limited once he took on the new role. In a way, offering such luxurious accommodations seemed almost like a bribe... Benefit? Bribe? Were they really all that different?

He thought about Claire's apartment above the laundromat—the one he'd glimpsed through the half-open office door, the cramped stairwell leading up to it, the hand-lettered sign that read "PRIVATE" as if anyone might accidentally wander up three flights of narrow stairs. He thought about the buttons she'd collected from her mother. The paper ledger she still used. The way she stretched a budget so thin you could see through it and somehow made it work.

Any one of these California houses could swallow her entire building. The parking garage of the Bay View property was probably bigger than her apartment. And here he was, about to go on a date with her, knowing he had a one-month countdown ticking in the background like a bomb he'd agreed to sit on.

This is selfish, he told himself. *You know you're leaving.*

You know she doesn't know. You know this is going to hurt someone, and it's probably going to be her.

He closed the housing PDF without selecting a preference.

I can't do this now. He walked away from his computer toward his closet, pushing several "meeting outfits" out of the way. He wanted to look nice to see Claire—but not *that* nice. A suit would be overkill.

As he browsed his wardrobe, he stopped to examine a dark gray, short-sleeved polo sweater. It was lightweight, and he knew it would look nice with his favorite pair of dark wash jeans. He pulled it out, held it against himself in the mirror, and wondered when the last time was that he'd been nervous about what to wear. College, maybe. Before he'd learned to weaponize clothes—the right suit for the right meeting, the right watch for the right client. Somewhere along the way, dressing had become strategy instead of expression.

Tonight, he didn't want strategy. He wanted to look like someone Claire would be glad she'd said yes to.

He thought about calling Ben for advice, then decided against it. Ben would tell Gia, Gia would tell Claire, and by the time he arrived at the laundromat, everyone in a three-block radius would know he'd needed help choosing a sweater. Small towns were efficient that way. He pulled it off the hanger, grabbed the pants, socks, and a pair of black boxer briefs from his drawers, then left the folded pile on his bed. He walked to the master bathroom to shower. *May as well start getting ready—can't focus on anything else, anyway!*

After emerging from the shower, James shaved the stubble from his face, leaving a well-trimmed beard. He styled his hair with a little bit of gel, splashed some cologne on, then put on the clothes he'd laid out, finishing off the look with his favorite watch and a belt that matched his new loafers.

Gazing in the full-length mirror, he smiled. "Not bad!" he said to himself, and Chaos barked in agreement. James laughed. "Well, thanks, little buddy. We'll see what Claire thinks, I guess." The dog's ears perked up at the mention of Claire's name—or maybe he imagined it. He shrugged.

"Listen, I need to leave you alone for a while. Don't cause any chaos, Chaos!" James said, squinting at his puppy. Chaos whined as James opened the door to the bathroom and gestured inside. "I'm sorry, but you know you need to stay in the bathroom where it's dog-proofed, but don't worry, I'll leave your food and water—and I won't be gone long. I can't buy another couch for you to chew up. That was a one-time thing."

James rolled his eyes, recalling the day he walked in after leaving Chaos alone for twenty minutes to find his couch shredded, foam everywhere, and Chaos sitting in the center of the mess.

Once Chaos entered the bathroom, James slipped a food and water dish in, then closed the door. "I'll see you in a little while!" he told his dog, then left with enough time to visit the florist near the laundromat.

May as well do this right.

Wardrobe Change

CLAIRE

Chapter 16

WHILE JAMES WAS ACROSS TOWN DEBATING sweaters, Claire was having her own wardrobe crisis. She turned the sign on the front of the laundromat door to 'closed' as she dashed around, trying to prepare for her date with James. *Ugh! Why did I tell him to pick me up at 7?! I have no time to get ready... and I hate all of my clothes!*

She'd been distracted all day. Three customers had noticed. One of them—Mrs. Patterson, who brought in the same beige cardigan every Tuesday like clockwork—had actually patted Claire's hand and said, "Honey, whoever he is, he's lucky." Claire had denied everything, which Mrs. Patterson accepted with the knowing smile of a woman who'd been married for forty-three years and could smell a crush from across a laundromat.

Walt had picked up on her energy, too. He'd been following her around the laundromat all afternoon, bumping his nose against her leg every time she stopped moving, as if to say, *I don't know what's happening, but I'm here for it.* At one point, she'd caught him sitting in front of the office mirror, staring at his own reflection. "Don't judge me," she told him. "You licked a dryer sheet this morning. You have no moral authority here."

She pondered for a moment. She took such good care of her clothes that it suddenly occurred to her how long it had been since she'd bought anything new. In fact, she probably owned more clothing for Walt than for herself—a dog holiday sweater here, a tropical t-shirt there—while her own wardrobe consisted of the same items she'd worn for almost a decade. She scoffed.

As she turned, planning to dig through the clothes she had just washed and dried, something hanging on the customer clothing rack in the office caught her eye. *Oh, I couldn't...* On the rack, a stunning red cocktail dress hung. It was relatively conservative as far as that type of dress was concerned, but the color alone gave it a sexy vibe. It was much more alluring than anything *she* owned.

The dress belonged to a regular customer she'd known since they were children, but they weren't close. Like much of the town, their parents had been friends. Bridget Hurley had a high-level position as an executive assistant at some big tech business nearby and often attended events and client meetings that required her to dress up. The dress had been cleaned and waiting for pickup for several weeks already, despite Claire reaching out to her on more than one occasion. *Maybe she forgot about it. I could wear it, re-wash it, and she'd never know...*

Claire knew it was wrong, but she desperately wanted to make a good impression on James. She took a gulp and reached for the dress, removing it from the hanger carefully and holding it up against her body. She stepped into the dress and moved to gaze at her reflection in the office mirror. The knee-length dress was a deep, sultry shade of crimson. Red, but not brash. Cabernet, not candy apples. It featured a modest neckline that revealed just the tops of her collarbones, giving it a quiet elegance. The fitted three-quarter length sleeves left her wrists bare, and the bodice hugged her body gently enough to show her curves off without broadcasting them or making it appear as if she was trying too hard.

But... above all, she loved the back. It was cut in a narrow V that dipped between her shoulder blades, stopping just shy of daring. There was nothing flashy. No sequins, no glitter—but the dress oozed confidence (and it fit as if it'd been made for her!) As she took in her reflection, she knew there was no going back. She was wearing the dress. *What could go wrong? I am a stain-fighting warrior. There's not much I can't fix!*

She continued using the mirror to touch up the makeup job she'd applied earlier to cull her anxiety over seeing James, then pinned her hair up in a gentle bun, allowing several tendrils to fall past her ears. *Wow,* she thought, as she took in her appearance. For the first time in years, she felt like a woman, not just a kid pretending.

The last time she'd dressed up like this had been for her father's memorial service. She pushed the thought away immediately, but it left its fingerprint on the moment—a reminder that the dress she was wearing didn't belong to her, that the woman in the mirror was playing a part, and that parts eventually end.

Stop it, she told herself firmly. *You're allowed to have one nice night. One. You're not betraying anyone by putting on a dress and going to dinner. Mom would want this. Dad would want this. And Walt certainly doesn't care as long as someone feeds him.*

She looked at herself one more time. The woman staring back looked confident, put-together, almost elegant. Claire leaned closer to the mirror and whispered, "Don't screw this up."

The woman in the mirror didn't look entirely convinced.

Suddenly, the bell jingled, and the front door opened.

"Whoa!" came James' confident voice as he took in the feminine form before him. "You look stunning! Breathtaking, even."

Claire blushed. "Thank you," she said, managing to avoid her usual response to a compliment, which was typically, "No, I don't," or similar. She stepped out of the office and closed the half-door behind her, shutting Walt in before he had a chance to greet James. She had given him a high-value chew bone to keep him occupied while she got ready, and it seemed it was still acting as the perfect distraction.

"You don't look so bad yourself," she said, smiling at James. He looked incredible. He smelled even better. His sweater clung to his biceps just right. *Stop drooling,* Claire told herself, trying to avoid staring at the man before her.

"We should go before Walt realizes you're here without Chaos," Claire said, moving toward the door and grabbing her purse.

"I think you're forgetting something," James said, grinning.

"Huh?" Claire asked, confused, as James pointed downward to Claire's bare feet.

"OH!" Claire blurted. "Oh my gosh, I forgot shoes!" As far as James knew, she meant she forgot to put her shoes on... but the truth of the matter was that she'd completely forgotten that in order to wear a *cocktail dress,* one must also have appropriate footwear. As it stood, all she had were sneakers or flip-flops. Sighing, she made a quick decision. *Flip-flops, it is. I'll fake an injury.*

Claire slinked back into the office and grabbed her simple, black flip-flops from behind the desk, slipping them onto her feet. *Thank goodness I just did my toenails the other day.* As she moved to leave the office again, Walt looked up from his chewing and tilted his head in confusion at Claire's transformation, then quickly returned to the task at hand.

"Be a good boy, Walt. I'll be back in a couple of hours," she told her dog, praying he wouldn't cause any issues while she was gone. As she stepped out of the office, James glanced down at her feet. He said nothing, but she noticed a faint smile playing at the corners of his lips. *He must think I'm crazy.*

Charmed to Table

~~

CLAIRE

Chapter 17

THE RESTAURANT WAS ONLY A TEN-MINUTE DRIVE, but Claire spent every second of it acutely aware of her flip-flops. She tucked her feet as far under the seat as possible, as if the floorboard might judge her.

James, to his credit, said nothing about them. He drove with one hand on the wheel and the other resting on the center console, close enough to touch hers but not quite touching. The car smelled like leather and cologne and something warm she couldn't name—maybe just him. The car itself was absurd. Sleek, black, and entirely too expensive for a man who couldn't keep coffee off his shirt. She ran her fingers along the stitching on the edge of her seat.

"Nice car," she said, aiming for casual.

"Thanks. It's the one thing I splurged on. Ben and I bond over them—he's got the same model."

"I know. Gia calls it his midlife crisis on wheels. He's thirty-two."

James laughed, and the sound filled the small space. Claire felt it in her chest. *Stop it. It's just a laugh. People laugh. It's a normal human function.*

When they pulled up to *Charmed to Table*, Claire's breath caught. She'd been hearing about the changes Gia and Ben had made, but she hadn't seen them firsthand. The exterior had been transformed—warm Edison bulbs strung between the old oak trees in the courtyard, a hand-painted sign replacing the corporate-looking one from the previous owners, and window boxes overflowing with herbs and trailing flowers that made the whole entrance smell like rosemary and something sweet.

"Wow," Claire whispered.

"Yeah," James agreed, staring at the building. "Ben mentioned they'd been working on the place, but this is something else."

James opened her door before she had a chance to reach for the handle. She stepped out carefully, hoping the dim lighting would conceal her footwear situation. No such luck.

"For the record," James said, glancing down as they walked toward the entrance, "the flip-flops are my favorite part of the outfit."

"Shut up."

"I'm serious. They say, 'I'm wearing a stunning dress,

but I could also sprint away from this date at any moment.' Very on brand."

Claire snorted. "If I were going to sprint, I'd have worn the sneakers."

"Good to know you considered it."

"I consider sprinting away from most social situations."

He held the door open for her. "And yet... here you are."

Here I am, she thought, stepping inside.

The interior of *Charmed to Table* was even more striking than the outside. Gia had clearly been the guiding hand—the space felt like walking into someone's most beautiful, most intentional dinner party. Exposed brick walls, mismatched vintage chairs that somehow looked cohesive, clusters of candles on every surface, and a long communal table down the center with smaller, more intimate tables tucked along the edges. The whole restaurant felt alive with the quiet hum of conversation and clinking glasses.

A hostess Claire didn't recognize led them to a corner table near the window, where the candlelight caught the edges of the glasses and made everything look softer. Claire sat down and immediately tucked her feet under her chair.

"You've really never been here?" James asked, looking around with genuine appreciation.

"I keep meaning to. Gia's been asking me to come in for months. But between the laundromat and Walt and..." She gestured vaguely at the air. "Life, I guess. I don't really go out much."

"At all?"

"I mean, I go to the grocery store. I go to the park. I go to the vet—more than I should, given Walt's track record." She picked up the menu and scanned it. "But dinner out? I honestly can't remember the last time."

James watched her over the top of his menu, and something in his expression shifted—not pity, exactly, but something adjacent. Something softer. "That's going to change," he said simply.

Claire looked up. "Is it?"

"It is. Starting tonight."

Before she could respond, a familiar voice interrupted from behind the kitchen window. "Is that Claire? CLAIRE!" Gia's face appeared, flour-dusted and beaming, through the pass. She disappeared, and seconds later, the kitchen door burst open.

"Oh my God, you finally came!" Gia rushed over and threw her arms around Claire, who laughed into her friend's shoulder. "And you brought..." Gia pulled back and looked at James with open, unsubtle curiosity. "Hi. I'm Gia. I own this place with Ben. Claire and I go way back."

"James," he said, extending a hand. "I've heard great things about the restaurant."

"Ben mentioned you," Gia said, shaking his hand while side-eyeing Claire in a way that communicated roughly forty-seven follow-up questions she was storing for later. "He said you'd probably be coming in soon. I just didn't know it would be with my favorite girl." She squeezed Claire's arm. "I'm sending out the tasting menu. No arguments. You're not ordering off the regular menu tonight."

"Gia, I can't afford—"

"On the house." Gia held up a hand. "First visit. House rules. Non-negotiable. Ben's been wanting to test these new dishes on real humans anyway, and I trust your palate more than the food critic from the county paper who thought aioli was a type of pasta."

Claire opened her mouth to protest again, but Gia was already gone, the kitchen door swinging behind her.

James raised an eyebrow. "She's a force."

"You have no idea. She once reorganized my entire office in forty-five minutes because she said the 'energy was off.' She wasn't wrong, honestly."

The food arrived in waves—small, beautiful plates that looked like art and tasted like someone had put their whole heart into every bite. There was a roasted beet salad with goat cheese and candied walnuts, a mushroom risotto that was somehow both earthy and delicate, a pan-seared fish with a sauce Claire couldn't identify but wanted to bathe in, and, finally, a dessert that involved dark chocolate, sea salt, and something caramelized that made her close her eyes.

"Oh my God," Claire murmured through the last bite. "I need to come here more often."

"You will. I'll make sure of it." James said it like a promise, not a suggestion, and something about the certainty in his voice made Claire's stomach flip for reasons that had nothing to do with the food.

Between courses, they talked. Not the careful, curated first-date version of talking—the real kind, where things slipped out that probably shouldn't have, at least not this early. James told her about growing up as the kid who was always the new kid—six schools by the time he graduated, parents who treated him like a suitcase, packed and unpacked according to their career itineraries.

"They weren't bad parents," he said, tracing the rim of his wine glass. "They just weren't particularly... present. They were always chasing the next thing. Bigger title, better city, fancier house. I think they assumed that if they kept moving, they'd eventually arrive somewhere that felt like enough." He paused. "I don't think they ever did."

"And you?" Claire asked carefully. "Do you feel like you've arrived?"

Something flickered behind his eyes. A hesitation so brief she almost missed it. He picked up his glass and took a slow sip before answering. "I'm starting to think arrival is less about where you are and more about who's there when you get there."

That was a dodge, Claire thought. A beautiful, poetic dodge, but a dodge nonetheless. She filed it away and didn't push. Not tonight.

"My parents were the opposite," she said instead. "They never left. Born here, married here, ran the laundromat here, died here." The last word landed harder than she intended, and she felt the familiar tightening in her chest. "Sorry. That got dark."

"Don't apologize."

"It's just—people don't usually want the dead-parents backstory on a first date. It kills the mood. Pun not intended." She winced. "Okay, pun a little intended. My dad would've appreciated it."

James didn't laugh, but his eyes crinkled. "What were they like?"

She hadn't expected the question to hit the way it did. People asked about her parents in the abstract—how long ago, was it sudden, how old was she—but almost no one asked what they were *like*. As if the logistics of death were more polite to discuss than the fact that two real people had existed and been loved.

"My mom was warm," Claire began, her voice quieter now. "Like, the kind of warm where you walked into the laundromat and felt like you'd walked into someone's living room. She knew everyone's name, everyone's kids' names, their dogs' names. She kept candy in a jar on the counter for the kids who came in. She played music—always oldies— and sometimes, if it was slow, she'd dance between the machines." Claire laughed softly. "She was ridiculous. In the best way."

She paused, running her thumb along the stem of her glass. "My dad was the handyman. He could fix anything. The machines, the plumbing, the sign out front, a kid's broken toy. He was quiet, but people trusted him. I think it was because he never tried to sell you anything. He just... showed up, and fixed things." Her voice caught slightly. "He would have liked you."

James was very still. "Why do you think that?"

"Because you show up." She shrugged, as if it were simple, even though it didn't feel simple at all. "Most people don't."

The silence that followed was the kind that didn't need filling. James reached across the table and placed his hand over hers. He didn't say anything. He didn't need to.

After a moment, Claire cleared her throat and straightened. "Okay. Enough sadness. Tell me something embarrassing about yourself. I need to recalibrate."

James tilted his head. "Define embarrassing."

"Something that would make me feel less mortified about the flip-flops."

"Fair enough. When I was twelve, I had a presentation in front of the entire school—my first week at a new school, mind you—and I was so nervous that I walked onto the stage, opened my mouth to speak, and immediately threw up into the microphone."

Claire's hands flew to her mouth. "No."

"Into. The. Microphone. It echoed."

She lost it. The laugh came out loud and graceless and entirely unprepared, the kind that turned heads at neighboring tables. She covered her face with both hands, her shoulders shaking.

"It gets worse," James continued, clearly enjoying himself. "The mic was attached to a portable speaker, so the sound of me puking was essentially amplified across the entire gymnasium. The janitor quit that day. Not because of the mess—he'd just been looking for a reason, apparently."

Claire was crying now, tears of laughter streaming down her face. "Stop. I can't breathe."

"So, in summary: you're wearing flip-flops to a nice restaurant. I once threw up at concert volume in front of three hundred strangers. I think we're even."

She wiped her eyes. "We are absolutely not even, but I appreciate the effort."

As the evening wound down and the restaurant began to empty, Claire noticed something she'd been trying not to notice all night: the way James's phone kept lighting up on the table beside his wine glass. He'd flipped it face-down early in the meal, but the screen still pulsed through the case—a persistent, rhythmic glow that he steadfastly ignored.

"You can check that, you know," she said. "I won't be offended."

"It's nothing," he said, a little too quickly. "Just work stuff."

"At nine-thirty on a weeknight?"

"My work doesn't really have hours. One of the perks and curses of consulting." He picked up the phone and silenced it completely, slipping it into his jacket pocket. "Tonight is about you. And me. And..." he gestured at the decimated dessert plate. "Whatever this chocolate situation was."

Claire let it go. But she noticed the tension that had crept into his jaw, the way his hand had tightened around the phone before pocketing it. *He's hiding something.* She pushed the thought down. *Everyone has things they're not ready to share on a first date. You literally just told him about your dead parents over risotto. Give the man some grace.*

"Thank you," she said as they stood to leave. "For tonight. For all of it."

James helped her with the light jacket she'd grabbed from behind the counter—one of her own, at least, not borrowed—and his fingers brushed the bare skin of her upper back where the dress dipped. She felt it everywhere.

"Thank *you*," he said. "For the flip-flops. For the stories. For..." He trailed off, searching for the right word.

"For being a mess?" she offered.

"For being real," he said. "I don't get a lot of real."

They walked out into the cool night air, and Claire tipped her head back to look at the sky, clear and full of stars. She felt warm and full and slightly terrified. Not of

James—of how much she already wanted this to keep going.

"So," James said, opening her car door. "I owe you a proper goodnight."

"You owe me a proper pair of shoes, honestly."

He laughed. And then he was close, closer than the car door required, his hand finding the small of her back where the fabric ended and her skin began. "Can I take you home?" he asked. "To the laundromat, I mean. To drop you off." He paused. "Unless…"

"Unless?" she echoed, her pulse doing something reckless.

"Unless you'd like to not be dropped off just yet."

Claire looked at him and made a decision that had nothing to do with logic and everything to do with the way her body felt like it was on fire and her mind felt, for once, completely quiet.

"Take me to the laundromat," she said. "But don't drop me off."

The drive back was short, charged with a current neither of them acknowledged out loud. James parked in front of *Dirty Laundry / Bubbles & Barks* and walked around to open her door. Claire stepped out and turned toward the entrance, fishing for her keys.

James opened the door for Claire. She walked through, then froze, realizing she hadn't locked it behind them earlier. Upon spinning around to lock up, she bumped directly into James, who caught her in his arms before she stumbled backward off the entrance step. Her first instinct was to pull away, but something caused her to linger, and his hold grew tighter as she glanced up at him.

"I... I forgot to lock the door," she said meekly, tilting her head to look down, trying to will herself to take a step back, but barely able to form words as his chest pressed against her.

James placed two fingers beneath her chin and lifted it so her gaze met his. "You know, we keep finding ourselves like this. Maybe the universe is trying to tell us something," he said, grinning.

"Like what?" Claire asked, placing her hand on his behind and squeezing. *Did I really just do that? Who am I? What has gotten into me? It must be the dress.*

"Judging from the placement of your hand, I think you have a pretty good idea what I mean..."

Claire didn't move. She struggled to find words as James traced a finger over her lips with a touch so light it was barely there. "I... I—"

"You want me to kiss you?" James whispered in her ear, then traced his lips down her neck so his lips were almost touching hers. She nodded slowly.

"Say it. Tell me you want me to kiss you," he demanded gently.

"Yes. I want you to kiss me," she breathed.

He hesitated.

"Please."

James pushed Claire gently against the still-unlocked front door, forcing it open and moving the two of them inside. Then, he leaned against it, using the weight of his body to close it before reaching an arm around to lock it. He continued to push against Claire, moving her toward the back of the laundromat, teasing her skin with his fingers and his breath.

"James," Claire exclaimed breathlessly. "Please!"

"Please, what?" he feigned ignorance, his face inches from hers.

"Kiss me," she repeated.

"As you wish," James finally conceded, bending slightly to put his lips against hers.

The Apartment

JAMES

Chapter 18

HOLY FUCK. THIS WOMAN IS GOING TO BE THE death of me. James felt like every one of his senses was on fire, as if Claire ignited his entire body and mind with her very presence. *And, oh my God—that dress!*

As his gaze wandered up and down her body, he couldn't make it another second without his lips on hers. With one hand against his back, and the other beneath her chin, he leaned down and tilted her head up, placing his mouth against hers and taking her lower lip in his teeth before allowing his tongue to gently enter and deepen the kiss. *Fucking Christ.*

His hand wandered from Claire's back down to the perfect curve of her ass, accentuated by the beautiful, sexy red dress. He pressed against her, pushing her body in even tighter against his, subtly commanding her to follow his lead—gentle but dominant. She did as he asked without any words between them.

Suddenly, Claire pulled away from the kiss.

"What's wrong?" mumbled James, desperately wanting to dive back into Claire's perfect mouth, but respecting her enough to make sure she was okay with everything. "Are you okay?"

Claire nodded. She stared into James' eyes, then tilted her head in the direction of a series of doors in the back of the laundromat. "Do you know where that middle door leads?" she asked, with what seemed like a teasing smile.

"Uh, storage?" James asked, unable to think clearly.

"Let me show you..." Claire said, pulling further away and taking James' hand to lead him in the direction of the doors.

She opened the center door, revealing a stairwell leading upward. James looked at her curiously, still uncertain of what could possibly be important enough for her to break *that* kiss. He followed as she moved up the stairs and opened the door at the top, stepping inside behind her.

Once beyond the door, James realized he was in an apartment. It was small, but clean and well-kept. His eyes wandered, noticing the dog dish labeled "WALT" in a small kitchen area off to one side. Suddenly, it hit him.

"Your... your... apartment?" he asked, sputtering in surprise. "I didn't know you—"

"Shhh..." Claire said, closing the door behind her. "I

know. I don't usually bring people up here." She leaned into him and whispered, "Where were we?"

The truth was, she never brought people up here. Not since her parents. This apartment was the one space that was entirely hers—the place where she cried and ate cereal for dinner and talked to Walt like he was a person and didn't have to perform competence for anyone. Bringing James into it felt like handing him a key to a room she'd kept locked for years.

But standing here, with the taste of him still on her lips and the warmth of his body pulling at hers like gravity, she didn't feel exposed. She felt something she hadn't felt in a long time: chosen. Not for her stain-removal skills or her community organizing or her ability to keep a failing business alive through sheer stubbornness. Chosen for the messy, imperfect, flip-flop-wearing version of herself that she usually kept hidden behind the counter.

If you're going to do this, she told herself, *be here for it. Don't perform. Don't deflect. Don't make a joke. Just... be in your body for once in your life.*

Swallowing hard, James regained some composure and wrapped an arm around her waist. "I think we were doing this," he said, returning his lips to hers and snaking his tongue back in her mouth.

Claire pulled away slightly, just enough to tease him with the pause. "Mmm, we were, weren't we? And... what were we going to do next?"

"Something like this," James said, reaching around the stunning red dress and unzipping the already low back a few more inches. He slipped a hand down to caress the perfect curves of her ass before pulling his hand from the dress and bending slightly to grab the hem. He lifted the dress up and over her head in one swift motion, then tossed it aside. Swept up in their desire, neither of them noticed where the dress landed. Not that they would have cared in that moment, anyway.

"You're absolutely beautiful," James whispered into her ear, kissing his way down her neck to her collarbone, across her chest, then down to her breasts.

And for the first time in as long as she could remember, Claire believed it. Not because he said it—men had said it before, in contexts that ranged from genuine to transactional. But because of the way he looked at her when the dress came off. There was no performance in his eyes. No calculation. Just a man seeing a woman and being undone by it, and a woman letting herself be seen without flinching.

She had expected to feel self-conscious. Her body wasn't the kind that graced magazine covers—she had the frame of a woman who lifted industrial laundry bags and chased a seventy-pound dog and sometimes forgot to eat lunch. She had a scar on her hip from a washing machine repair gone wrong. Her hands were perpetually dry from detergent and hot water. These were the things she noticed when she looked at herself.

But James wasn't looking at any of those things. Or maybe he was, and they didn't matter, or maybe they mattered in a way she hadn't considered—as evidence of a life lived fully, in a body that worked hard and carried things and showed up every day. Whatever he saw, it made his breath catch, and that was enough.

Be here, she told herself again. *Just be here.* He held one in his hand as he brought his lips around it, nibbling slightly with his teeth, then sucking the nipple, feeling it harden in his mouth as he teased her body.

Claire groaned with desire and reached for the hardness she felt rubbing against her through James' pants. She gripped his bulge and moved her hand up and down against it, the friction through his pants driving James to moan.

"Fuck," James said, pulling away from Claire's perfect tits for a moment. "You're driving me fucking crazy."

"The... feeling... is... mutual." Claire struggled to get the words out as James moved to the opposite breast, repeating his licking, nibbling, and sucking on the other side.

When James couldn't take another moment of his cock being stroked, but still contained by his boxer briefs and pants, he mumbled to Claire, "Bedroom?"

She nodded and led him to her bedroom door, then across the room to her bed, where he gently guided her backward until she fell onto her bed into a sitting position. He gripped her panties with two fingers and pulled them over her ankles, tossing them aside, and admired her perfectly trimmed pussy.

He trailed a finger from her mouth, moving slowly down her body, over each nipple, still sensitive from their stimulation a few moments prior, over her stomach, and to her lower abdomen. As he made his way downward, Claire reached for his sweater, pulling it over his head and placing her hands on his chest, which was more muscular than she'd anticipated. "Mmmm," Claire muttered as she pinched a nipple, her body rising at the hips, urging James further downward.

"Patience, Princess," James said, still teasing just away from her mound. "Good things come to good girls who wait..." he smirked.

Claire groaned and tugged at his belt, unhooking the latch as he continued to torture her, tracing just above and beside the places she most wanted him to touch. As she began to pull his jeans downward, James surprised her, pressing a finger against her clit and rubbing slowly but firmly as he pushed her gently down into a prone position, her legs hanging slightly off the bed.

"Oh my God," Claire said, "Oh my GOD!" James stepped out of his loosened pants and pulled his boxer briefs off, while keeping one hand on Claire. His cock sprang from its constraints, thick. Claire started to sit up to reach for him, but he gently pushed her back. He knew he was relatively well endowed, but he wasn't ready to have Claire's full attention yet. He had other things in mind first. He continued to rub her as he placed the fingers of his other hand gently against her slit. He looked up at her, his eyes asking permission.

"Is this okay?" he asked.

"Mmm, mmhmm. Mmhmm."

"Say it. Tell me."

"It's okay."

"What's okay? What do you want me to do?" James traced his fingers up and down along her slit, waiting for her to ask him to enter, teasing her body and feeling her wetness. "Fuck, Claire. You're dripping."

"I want your fingers inside me. I want to feel you touching me inside."

James groaned as he shoved several fingers inside Claire, curved them, and rubbed her from within. Her hips rose to meet his fingers, begging him to go deeper. He began thrusting his fingers in and out of Claire's pussy, meeting her grinding motions, until she couldn't take it anymore. With one hand massaging her clit and the other inside her, she pushed her hips hard against him. His curled fingers hit her most sensitive areas, and she moaned as her body clenched tight, an orgasm erupting over her. Pleasure washed over her in waves until, finally, her body relaxed.

James pulled his fingers from inside her and kissed her deeply.

"Did you like that, good girl?"

"Mmmhmm," Claire mumbled as she reached for James, grabbing his cock and rubbing it up and down. James didn't think it was possible, but it made him even harder. "I want to feel you inside me. All of you. I want you to fill me," Claire said, not wasting any time with gentle words.

James sucked in a breath deeply. "Are you sure?"

"Yes. God, yes. Please."

James reached his hand back down toward his jeans on the floor and pulled his wallet from his pocket, grabbing a condom and unrolling it over his dick. He lifted Claire's legs, where they hung at the side of the bed, and rotated them—and the rest of her body—effectively tossing her onto the bed the rest of the way. He crawled toward her, bringing his mouth to hers and kissing her hard.

"You sure this is what you want?" he asked.

"Yes," Claire said breathlessly.

"Yes, what?"

"Yes. I want you inside me."

"Say please, Princess."

"Pleeeeaaassseee," she growled, desperate to feel his cock inside her, stretching her, filling her. "Please be inside me, now. Please let me feel you inside me," Claire begged.

James couldn't handle another moment of waiting or teasing. He lined himself up with Claire's pussy and rubbed his cock against it several times before pushing inside her. He filled her deeply, thrusting gently at first, then harder as her hips rose to meet his thrusts.

"Oh my God, Claire. You feel so fucking good," James

said, trying desperately to keep himself from coming too soon. It had been a while, after all.

Claire wrapped her legs around James' torso, effectively pulling him even deeper inside her. They rocked together as one, their breathing matching in intensity and rhythm.

"Turn over," James said abruptly, pulling out of Claire's body.

"Huh?" Claire asked, likely unable to process the words in the heat of the moment.

"Over," he said, gesturing in a circular motion, indicating for her to turn and get on her hands and knees in front of him. "I want to take you from behind, Princess."

Claire nodded and, without further prompting, rolled onto her knees and rested on her forearms, lifting her ass into the air and giving it a little wiggle.

"Good girl," James said, smirking and watching the expression of desire and relief cross her face as he pushed inside her again, fucking her hard from behind.

Fulfilled

CLAIRE

Chapter 19

"Mmm, you can't say that to me," Claire managed to say in between gasps. She didn't care about maintaining any semblance of feminine grace at that moment. She wanted good sex. She needed it. Dirty, rough sex. And James was *not* one to disappoint, apparently.

What she found surprising was how comfortable she felt with James. She wasn't usually one to be particularly open sexually, especially with someone she didn't even know very well. It's not that she was a prude, but it usually took her a while to open up. With him, she felt uninhibited and free. She felt *desirable,* even with her flaws.

"I don't think you're in any position to tell me what I can and can't say," James teased, pulling out for a moment and leaving her empty. "Do you?"

Claire groaned. "Say whatever you want, just don't stop."

James grabbed her hair and gave it a tug as he re-entered her. "Anything you say, good girl," he said as he gripped her hips and pulled her into his thrusts. They continued this way for several more minutes, switching positions multiple times, exploring the magic of how their bodies fit together and moved as one. This was *not* awkward, first-time sex.

Finally, as they returned to their original placement, with James on top of her, gazing into her eyes as they moved as one, their passion reached a peak. As she neared another orgasm, Claire clung to James, burying her face in his chest and clenching him tightly with her legs, wanting him as deep inside of her as possible. She didn't want to let go, she didn't want it to end, but she wanted to feel him release, to know that she'd given him the same pleasure he'd already given her... soon to be twice.

She could tell he was close. As Claire's climax crashed over her, she moaned, "I'm coming. Oh my God, I'm coming so hard for you!"

It sent James right over the edge. "Fuuuuuck," he groaned, thrusting deeply inside her as he jerked several times. He collapsed against her body, resting his head against her chest as he recovered his breath—and the ability to speak.

Claire lay in the dark afterward, listening to James breathe. His arm was draped across her stomach, heavy and warm. The apartment was quiet except for the distant hum of the laundromat machines running their overnight cycles —a sound she'd fallen asleep to for three years, a sound that usually meant loneliness but tonight meant something different.

She turned her head to look at him. In sleep, the charm fell away. The confidence, the easy grin, the quick wit—all of it softened into something younger and more vulnerable. He looked, she thought, like a man who'd been running for a long time and had finally stopped.

Don't do this, the cautious part of her whispered. *Don't make him into a home. You know what happens to homes.*

But the rest of her—the part that had danced to Motown in an empty laundromat, that had thrown a coin in a fountain and wished for someone to stay, that had put on a borrowed red dress and chosen flip-flops because she didn't know how to be anyone other than who she was— that part whispered back: *Too late.*

After a while, James stirred. He rolled over to lie beside Claire on his side, taking her in. He wrapped an arm around her, tracing a finger up and down her arm. "Wow," he said. "I... uh... I didn't plan to... uh—"

"Yeah... Same," Claire said, understanding without any further explanation. However, a thoughtful look crossed over her face, and the peace she'd felt a moment ago faltered. *I hope I didn't mess up something that could have been more by being... too easy.*

James noticed the slight change in her demeanor and shifted to rest his head on his arm, propped up on his elbow. He looked at her for a long moment, then said, "I'm not going anywhere, you know. Unless you want me to."

A look of relief crossed her face. *He's not leaving.* Claire grinned. "I mean... I could probably be convinced to let you stay."

James leaned forward and kissed her on the mouth, this time gently, sweetly. Claire kissed back, then pushed him away as the kiss grew more intense.

"That's precisely what got us into this situation!" she said, doing a ninja roll off the bed and quickly grabbing a blanket from the nearby chair to cover up. *Somehow, nakedness is so much easier in the heat of the act!* She padded toward the other room to retrieve the borrowed dress before it wrinkled beyond saving—some habits die hard, even post-sex. James rose and grabbed the various articles his outfit had previously included.

As Claire neared the vicinity of the entry, where she'd thrown the dress off in the throes of passion, she sniffed the air. *Bleach? Oh, right.* She'd been trying to get a tough stain out the night before, and she'd left the bleach-covered rag resting in a small container of chemicals on the table by the door, planning to bring it down to the—

"OH MY GOD!" Claire shouted as her eyes shifted to the table, the borrowed dress draped over the surface, resting on the bleach-covered rag. Her eyes filled with horror. Laundry lesson number... She didn't know or care what number it was—*there's no coming back from bleach!*

She dashed over to the table and lifted the dress, examining the fabric with tears in her eyes as James appeared in just his jeans, having left the bedroom in a hurry to check on her after her outburst. "Is everything okay?" he asked.

"No... I... I..." Claire held up the dress, showing a yellow-white stain, then gesturing to the table and the post-it note she had taped to the container: **BLEACH.**

"Oh, shit." James winced. It seemed that even a laundry novice like him knew that bleach and an expensive dress are a bad combination. "Can it be fixed? You're the expert, surely you can fix it?"

Claire shook her head, at a loss for words. Finally, she muttered, "No. Not bleach. It's not salvageable. And, even worse... It's not actually *mine*." She groaned and rested her head in her hands, inadvertently causing the blanket to slip off.

Great. Now I'm standing here naked, holding a ruined dress that I can't afford to replace with a man I'll probably never see again, given that I'm now the girl who is standing in the living room crying after sex.

James took the dress from Claire and set it back on the table, covering the bowl of bleach once again. He wrapped his arms around her and pulled her away from the garment. "I'll replace it," he said. "One laundry favor for another, you know?"

"I can't let you do that. Trust me, this is going to be a VERY expensive laundry favor," Claire said, allowing herself to rest her head against his chest. *If I'm never going to see him again anyway, I may as well let myself be comforted now...*

"I'm not worried about the money," he said. "Come on. Let's try to find the dress." He grabbed his phone and reached over to take a photo of the inner tag for the size, brand, and other information. "Bedroom. Go," he said, picking up and passing her the blanket before ushering her back to her room.

He tucked her into the bed before climbing in next to her and wrapping his arm back around her. On his phone, he zoomed in on the information printed on the tag, then began typing into a search engine, trying to find the exact dress either locally or for quick delivery.

His jaw dropped as images of the cocktail dress appeared on the screen of his phone, alongside prices. "Wow," he said, chuckling.

"What?" asked Claire, glancing at his phone. "Oh my God. Over three thousand dollars for one dress?! Who has that?!" She groaned. "I'm so screwed."

"No, you're not," James replied. "I told you. I've got this. It's my fault. Both of our faults, anyway. So, we'll handle it. We'll order one, and it will be here within a few days... Whose is it, anyway?"

Claire winced. "A client—Bridget Hurley."

James sputtered. "I'm sorry..." He cleared his throat. "Did you say Bridget Hurley?"

"Yeah, she works at some tech firm around here. I borrowed it because... well, I didn't have anything to wear tonight. I wanted to look nice." Claire buried her face in her hands, wishing she could disappear. She expected James to walk out—too much drama for a one-night stand! Instead, when she looked at him, he was grinning.

"You're telling me you borrowed a dress worth several thousand dollars because you had nothing to wear on a date with little old me?" he smirked.

Claire rolled her eyes. "Something like that. I know. It was dumb. God, I'm so stupid!"

"No," James started. "It was sweet... and as far as the dress is concerned. Don't worry about it. I'll handle it. I'll handle Bridget, too."

Claire eyed James. "You... you know her? Oh my God. You *KNOW* her?!" Claire's face blushed a shade of pink she didn't know was even possible.

James grinned. "I do. You could say I have dealings with her boss... and they both want something from me pretty badly right now. I'll make sure she gets an explanation *and* a new dress—and it'll be my fault. Don't you worry your pretty little head."

Claire lifted her head from his chest, tears forming in

her eyes once again—but this time it was over the kindness of a man she'd only just met. "What... What will you tell her?" she asked.

James reached over and wiped a tear that had made its way down her cheek, then placed his finger on her lips. "Shhh. I told you. Don't worry about it. I'll figure something out. Maybe I was doing laundry in the laundromat and tripped, spilled bleach all over the dress? Maybe I'll blame Chaos. Who knows? Regardless, I'll figure it out— and she'll get her dress. The same one, or better. I have a lot of connections, believe it or not." He winked.

Who is this man?! What kind of connections? Claire stared at James.

Spin Cycle

CLAIRE

Chapter 20

THE MORNING ARRIVED, PALE SUNLIGHT
filtering through the slats of Claire's blinds, turning the
mess on the table into a crime scene—bleach rag, ruined
dress, two cups that had once held courage disguised as
coffee. James was still there, sitting on the edge of the couch
in a t-shirt and jeans, elbows on his knees, scrolling through
his phone like it owed him a miracle.

For a few seconds, Claire pretended to be asleep. It gave
her a buffer between the warmth of last night and the cold
reality of the daylight outside—and her current predica-

ment. Her body remembered everything so vividly. His hands, the laughter, the way she'd forgotten to be self-conscious in his presence. But the sharp smell of bleach in the air was a reminder that nothing washes completely clean.

She let herself study him while he thought she was sleeping. He looked different in the morning light—less polished, more human. His hair, so carefully styled last night, had surrendered to sleep and stuck up at odd angles. There was a crease on his cheek from her pillowcase. He'd rolled his jeans up at the ankles at some point in the night, and she noticed, absurdly, that even his feet were attractive. *Get a grip, Claire.*

What struck her most, though, was how out of place he looked in her apartment. Not because he was uncomfortable—he seemed perfectly at ease, legs stretched out, phone balanced on one knee. But the contrast was almost laughable. This was a man who drove a car that cost more than everything Claire owned combined. A man who'd peeled five hundred dollars off a wad of cash like it was loose change. And here he was, in her three-hundred-square-foot apartment above a laundromat, sitting on a couch she'd inherited from her parents that had a permanent dog-hair sheen and one cushion that sagged in the middle.

The apartment was clean—Claire was physically incapable of tolerating a mess that wasn't Walter-generated—but it was small. One bedroom, a kitchen that doubled as a hallway, a bathroom where you could touch opposing walls if you stretched your arms out, and a living area that functioned as office, dining room, and Walt's secondary bedroom. Every surface held evidence of a life lived in tight quarters: stacked mail on the counter, a laundry basket she used as an end table, framed photos of her parents crowded onto a single shelf because there wasn't room for them anywhere else.

She wondered if he noticed. She wondered if it mattered. She wondered if he was comparing it to wherever he lived—probably somewhere with actual closet space and countertops that didn't double as ironing boards.

Stop it, she told herself. *He's still here. He stayed. That means something. Or it means he fell asleep and hasn't escaped yet.* She pushed the thought away, but it left a residue, like bleach on fabric—invisible until you looked for it.

He looked up when Claire shifted under the blanket. "Morning," he said quietly, voice still rough with sleep. He'd stayed. Against all logic, as far as she was concerned, he'd stayed.

"Morning," Claire managed. Her voice cracked like it hadn't decided whether to sound casual or mortified.

James held up his phone. "Good news and bad news. The good news is that Bridget is very easily reachable. The bad is that, well, she's... Bridget. But I'm handling it."

Claire sat up, clutching the blanket tighter. "You shouldn't have to."

"Claire, it's a dress. I've made costlier mistakes."

"It's *her* dress. A dress I should never have put on in the first place." She pulled the blanket tighter, as if it could insulate her from the reality of the situation. The morning light was merciless—it showed every wrinkle, every stain, every consequence of the night before in high definition. "Three thousand dollars, James. I saw it on your phone last night. Three thousand dollars for a dress I put on because I wanted to look nice for you, and now it's ruined because I left a bleach rag out like an amateur."

The number sat between them like a third person in the

room. Three thousand dollars. That was more than her monthly revenue on a good month. That was the dryer repair she'd been putting off. That was three months of Walt's food and vet bills. That was a number that belonged to a different life—Bridget's life, James's life—not hers. And the ease with which he'd barely reacted last night when the price appeared on screen—*no visible flinch, no sharp intake of breath, just calm scrolling*—made her stomach twist.

He shrugged. "Then it's my problem, too, for knowing her and being involved."

"You really think you can fix everything so easily?"

He smiled a little. "Professionally? That's literally my job."

"And personally?" Claire asked, before she could stop herself.

His smile faded into something softer. "Personally... let's just say I'm still learning. But, I can fix this. Trust me."

Claire and James sat there in the quiet hum of morning. It was the kind of silence that felt like it was still choosing which direction to fall, calm or chaos. Walt's snoring from the other room filled the space between them.

"Do you need to go?" Claire finally asked.

He hesitated, then nodded. "I should. The sooner I smooth this out, the better."

Claire nodded. She wanted to say: *Stay.* She wanted to say: *Forget Bridget. Forget the dress.* Instead, she gathered the blanket around herself like armor and said, "Thank you. For... not running."

He stood, tugged on his shoes, and gave Claire a look that made it hard to breathe. "For the record, I've never once wanted to run from you." Then he grinned, trying to lighten the load of his words. "Except maybe when you talk about stain removal with that intense glint in your eye. I feel like that's when your psycho shows through..."

"That's fair."

He leaned down and brushed a kiss across Claire's forehead. It was too gentle to be casual, but too brief to be worth overthinking, which she knew she'd do anyway. He grabbed the dress from the back of the chair, folded it into the garment bag Claire had set beside it, and tucked it under his arm. "I'll call you later," he said.

When the door shut behind him, the apartment was silent. Claire sat on the couch, wrapped in the blanket, remembering how the bleach stain looked almost like a heart—an uneven, accidental heart that wasn't going anywhere.

Claire sighed, then whispered to no one, "Guess we're both unfixable now," and went to start the coffee.

While the coffee brewed, she surveyed the damage. The bleach rag still sat on the table, and the faint chemical smell lingered in the air. The chair where the dress had been was empty—James had taken it with him, along with the problem and, apparently, a piece of her composure.

Can he fix this? The question surfaced unbidden, and she wasn't sure if "this" meant the dress or the feeling in her chest or the growing suspicion that she was falling for someone at a speed that defied every self-preservation instinct she'd developed over the past three years.

She poured the coffee, took a sip, and burned her tongue. *Perfect. Great start.* Walt padded over and leaned his full weight against her legs. She reached down and scratched behind his ears.

"It's just you and me, buddy. Like always." But even as she said it, the words felt less true than they had a week ago. Something had shifted. The apartment felt different—not empty, exactly, but aware of the space where someone else had been.

She finished the coffee, got dressed, and went downstairs to open the laundromat. The machines were waiting, patient and familiar. The detergent wall needed restocking. A wash-and-fold order was due by noon. These were things she understood. These were things she could control.

It was going to be a long day.

Damage Control

JAMES

Chapter 21

THE SMELL OF BLEACH FOLLOWED HIM INTO THE car, a constant reminder of the events the night before. James cracked the window, letting the cleansing air rush in as he tried not to picture Claire's face when she first saw the ruined dress. He was good at fixing things. The trick would be fixing this without making *her* feel like something that needed to be fixed.

Traffic crawled. He used the red lights as opportunities to conduct triage operations. Bridget first, then the boutique cleaner three blocks down that owed him a favor for migrating their business software from 'post-it notes' to something with an actual login. Worst case, he would buy Bridget a replacement; best case, the stain would be vanquished, and no one would need to know an impulsive midnight decision had met its match in household chemicals.

"Right, buddy?" he asked the empty passenger seat before remembering Chaos was at home, blissfully incapable of ruining couture—or hearing his words. "Right," he told himself.

He had to stop by *T.M. Enterprises* to assess a software issue that day, and it offered the perfect opportunity to assess Bridget's mood. When he arrived, the lobby smelled like lemon oil and money. Bridget Hurley materialized behind the reception desk with her sharp bob and sharper eyes, a tablet tucked under one arm, and a power suit that made 'executive assistant' sound like a technical term for "chaos coordinator for billionaires."

"There you are," she said, her smile crisp. "Mr. Marzini wants the Santa Clara housing packet in his, actually *my*, inbox by EOD. Also... uh... new hairstyle?"

He glanced past Bridget into the massive mirror situated on the wall beyond her desk. He'd changed into a dark sweater that announced nothing, but apparently the bleach in his hairline revealed enough. "It's a long story," he mumbled under his breath.

Her eyebrows did a synchronized lift. "Do I want to know?"

"No," he said. "Actually, yes, but not until after I fix it. I need ten minutes alone. I'm commandeering your conference room," he said, already moving. "I'll handle the software issue right after."

Bridget followed, appearing both amused and intrigued

despite herself. "If you turn my Tuesday into some new sort of chaos, I'm commandeering a portion of your new salary as compensation. I deal with enough as it is here." Then, she turned and walked out without further inquiry.

The conference room was situated behind glass walls, giving it an expansive view of the park below. James locked the door and placed the red dress on the table in its garment bag, about as innocent as a bomb. He unzipped the bag and groaned. The stain had dried to a shape a romantic might misinterpret as a heart, and a realist would call proof.

"Okay," he breathed, rolling up his sleeves. "Pre-soak wasn't possible. Gentle agitation. Cold water. No dryer. And then we pray to the dirty laundry gods." Claire's voice echoed in his head, practical and a little smug—*You blot. You do not scrub.*

He texted the cleaner: **Emergency! Thirty minutes? I'll tip like I mean it.**

The dots danced. **Bring it. Back door.**

"Bridget," he called through the door. "I need to run out... A bit of an emergency."

"You're lucky you're charming," she said. "Also, Mr. M asked me to remind you: *We are excited to welcome you to California.* His emphasis, not mine. And he expects those housing forms to appear in our inboxes STAT!"

"Noted." The word STAT landed heavy.

Five minutes later, James was merging into traffic again, the garment bag sitting like a witness (or perhaps the victim of a crime of passion!) in the back. He did not, under any circumstances, allow himself to think about Claire under the blanket, hair rumpled by sleep, insisting she could solve this alone because that was easier than letting someone stay. There was no time for that type of distraction at a time like this.

When he arrived, the boutique cleaner's back door was halfway open, held in place with a brick of cement. He hip-checked it open enough to pass through and was greeted by the hiss of steam and a man with the patience of a monk who had spent twenty years removing evidence. "What is it today?" the cleaner asked, glancing at the garment bag.

"Pride," James said, then amended, "And bleach."

The man winced visibly. "Bleach is... complicated," he said, peering at the stain. "You can't just put color back where it has been removed."

"I know." His stomach sank. "Is there any chance you could make this look like it was... meant to be there?"

The cleaner considered him over the rim of his bifocals. "On a runway? Yes, probably. At a cocktail party with men who have wives with opinions? Not a chance." He tapped the fabric. "We can try to soften the edge to make it less of a billboard-obvious bleach stain. But you'll definitely need a backup in case we only make it worse... which is always a possibility, no matter how good you are—and I'm very, very good."

"On it." James pulled out his phone and looked up the phone number to Cynthia, the woman who owned a small clothing boutique two blocks over. He hoped this was where the original had been purchased—and in a small town, it was highly likely, unless it had been special-ordered online. When the shopkeeper answered, he wasted no time and immediately asked for the same dress, same size, same shade of 'red that knew you were looking.'

"You owe me pie," Cynthia said. "And you're lucky we've been friends as long as we have. It'll be ready in twenty—and I expect to hear this story in its entirety sometime soon."

"Absolutely. Just not today! Thanks, Cyn. I owe you. I promise, the best pie I can get my hands on!" He ended the call and exhaled. "Okay." He glanced at the cleaner. "Softer edges, rush order. I'll be back."

Back in the car, he hovered over Claire's name on his phone's contact list. *I've got this,* he wanted to text. *You don't have to carry it alone.* It felt simultaneously like the truth and something too big to send before lunch.

Instead, he typed: **Running an errand. How is your day going?**

Her reply arrived before the next light: **Walt is working on his napping technique. I'm making a list of things bleach should never, ever meet.**

He smiled, then sobered as he pulled into the boutique. Inside, the owner presented the twin dress with the reverence of a sacrament. "If this is for Bridget Hurley, tell her she still owes me for the last time she 'borrowed' a gown for an event and returned it smelling like champagne and bad choices."

"I got it. Put it on my card," he said, handing her his credit card.

Cynthia, the shop owner narrowed her eyes. "Oh, I *definitely* have to hear *this* story…"

"Later. Promise." He hesitated, then added, "Also, entirely unrelated, but do you know anyone who'd sponsor dog treats for a park event? I'm trying to impress a woman by improving municipal morale and participation," he confessed.

Cynthia chuckled. "Reach out to Gia at the farm-to-table restaurant and the coffee shop. Gia is a great cook, and I know she's tried her hand at homemade dog treats as well. And, I'll toss in a gift card to the shop for the raffle."

By noon, James had the softened-edge original gown at the cleaner's and a brand-new backup in his car's trunk. He texted Bridget: **Solution incoming + security deposit of my dignity. Ten minutes.**

Back at T.M., Bridget had carved out five minutes between three impossible meetings. He laid both dresses on the table like a magic trick he hoped wouldn't lead to anyone being sawed in half. "Okay," James said. "Option A: your original dress with a stain so faint you have to *really* want to see it. Option B: a crisp, new replacement, identical."

He met her eyes. "Your call. And before you ask... don't, and I will return the favor in the form of never being late to or unable to attend anything you schedule for the rest of my natural life."

Bridget eyed both gowns, running a fingertip along the hem of Option A, then Option B. She looked up, unreadable. "You do realize this is above and beyond the call of... literally anything that involves impressing a woman?"

"I ruined your dress," he said. "I played a role in its destruction, anyway. Either way, it's my issue to solve."

She watched him for a few moments, something like

understanding cutting through the office sheen. "Option B," she decided finally. "Keep A as a client sample. It'll survive on a mannequin... or give it to *a friend*." She smirked. "And James?"

"Hmm?"

"Thank you. I won't ask how this happened..." She cleared her throat and straightened up, as if the gratitude and understanding had come out before she'd authorized it. "... because I don't care. You fixed it. Also, enjoy Santa Clara. It's a different kind of beautiful."

There it was, the sentence that made his chest feel two sizes too small. "Right," he said lightly. "Sunshine, innovation, and rents that could feed small villages."

She smiled, all business again. "Lucky for you, housing is on the house. Your orientation packet will arrive tonight. Flights are on hold for next week. Tell your dog he's a coastal elite now."

James nodded, gathered the garment bag, and headed toward the elevator. In the lobby, he paused long enough to text Claire a picture of the gift card from Cynthia's boutique. **For the Yappy Hour raffle. Consider it bribery.**

Her reply arrived with a photo of Chaos asleep on Walt's paw. **Bribery accepted. I offer my most sincere thanks... and Walt says you're tolerable.**

James laughed out loud. **Oh, stop. That dog loves me.** Then, for a second, he just stood there with his thumb on her name, feeling the decisions line up—California, job titles, a woman who pre-treats stains and might even help treat his bad habits if he let her. The elevator dinged again. Finally, an easy decision. He chose the door and stepped out.

On the drive back toward town, he told himself he was

stopping by the laundromat to return a garment bag and drop off a gift card. He did not tell himself he was going to see if the space between them felt the same when the sun was up, and there were witnesses.

He parked. He took a breath. He told his heart to behave. And then he went in.

Permits and Problems

CLAIRE

Chapter 22

THE DAYS SINCE THE DRESS DISASTER HAD TAKEN on a rhythm Claire hadn't expected—and wasn't sure she trusted. James texted her every morning, sometimes just a photo of Chaos doing something ridiculous, sometimes a question about her day that made it clear he'd actually been listening the day before. She caught herself smiling at her phone more than once, then immediately scolding herself for it. *It's been a week, Claire. Get it together.*

Still, she couldn't deny that having someone in her corner felt different from anything she'd experienced in years. Not better, necessarily. Just... different. Lighter. Like someone had taken one of the heavy bags she'd been carrying and slung it over their own shoulder without asking.

By late afternoon, the laundromat had settled into its steady hum—the sound of other people's messes and to-do lists getting smaller. Claire had already mopped twice, reorganized the detergent wall once, and made a to-do list so long it looked like a cry for help written in bullet points. Walt lay on the cool tile like a felled tree, motionless unless sound caught his attention.

And, it did. As the bell over the door chimed, James stepped in carrying a garment bag and an envelope in his outstretched hand, like a man trying to bribe fate with offerings.

"Special delivery," he said, holding up the bag. "One dress, morally and mostly aesthetically redeemed. And—now, yours." He held up the gift card. "One pretty significant gift card to Cynthia's to help support a community event I hear is going to save the town's collective soul."

Claire stood there with a Sharpie in her hand and a thousand feelings she had no time to sort out before she spoke. "You did it." It came out softer than she meant. She coughed it into something brisk. "Good. Great. I mean, thank you."

He set the bag on the counter and glanced at her list. "Permit map, waste station, vendor replacement, volunteer schedule..."

"Don't read my secrets." She grinned, sliding the paper upside down and toward herself. "They're mostly begging and tape, anyway."

"Begging and tape are the cornerstones of civilization, in case you hadn't heard." He nodded at the dress. "Bridget took a replacement. The cleaner softened the other. It's not perfect... but it's yours if you want it. And, with the way it looks on you, I strongly suggest you keep it." He smiled.

"Mine?" she asked, letting out a chuckle because the alternative was crying. "I've never owned anything like this before...."

He tilted his head, studying her like he was trying to decide which version of her had shown up today. "Now you do. Again, the stain is still there, but not as noticeable, and maybe you can blend it even more. Plus, it comes with a good story." James winked, then studied her for a moment. "You look tired. How are you?"

"Busy," she said. "And possibly made entirely of coffee at this point."

"Permission to assist? I have to get back to the office at some point to fix a software issue, but I do have some time."

She opened her mouth to say the usual no, then closed it. The word tasted different after last night. "You can... you can help me stack the load of linens from out of the big dryers in the back and pretend you work here while I call some of the vendors who haven't paid their table fees?"

"On it." He passed behind her, careful to give her space and not crowd the air between them. Somehow, despite the chaos they'd endured, he still smelled like clean cotton... and a day spent outrunning problems.

Her phone buzzed. Tina: *Need revised layout now. Council wants clearer buffer zones. And a second waste station.*

She texted back: *On it.*

James returned, dusting dog hair off his sweater like an initiation ritual. "Stopped at the door to say hi to Walt. I barely even touched him," he chuckled, gesturing to the fur as he saw the look of concern cross her face. "So, what's the latest?"

"Buffer zones and waste station issues. Also, my dog-treat vendor bailed." She tapped the list with the Sharpie. "I can do this. I just need... time. And a clone."

"Might be able to help with dog treats. I was actually doing some research on that exact topic earlier. Have you asked Gia?"

"Oh my God. Gia! Why didn't I think of that?! I've just been so busy, it didn't even occur to me. Of course! She went through that phase where she was all into homemade dog treat recipes! Walter was her guinea pig. How the hell did you come up with that?"

"I have to keep *some* secrets... What you need is a team. I hear those are trendy."

"But I don't really have—"

Before Claire could finish speaking, the door chimed again. Dennis walked in carrying a folding table under one arm and a bin of neatly labeled supplies under the other. He wore his veterinary scrubs and emitted that steady, good-man energy that made people confess things about their pets and their lives in the same breath without even realizing it.

"Did someone say team?" he asked, setting the table down with a practiced thud. "I'm here with everything I need to act as your mobile-vet booth, as promised. Vaccines, nail trims, and even a water bowl for dramatic drinkers. Also, I brought sign-up sheets and a cash box I once used at a bake sale that nearly started a small war. You haven't lived until you've tried my chocolate chip cookies."

"Dennis." Relief loosened something in Claire's shoulders. "You're a miracle. Thank you. We can store it all in the back room until the event."

He gave her a lopsided grin. "Technically, I'm just a man with a veterinary degree, a table, and a cooler. But I'll take it." Then he noted James standing by the counter and offered a nod. "Hey, man."

"Hey," James returned, and something in the ease of the exchange told Claire she'd missed a chapter. The two of them seemed... fine. More than fine, actually.

She glanced between them. "Am I the only one who's being weird about this?"

"Yes," they said in unison.

"Speak for yourself," Dennis said, a smile sneaking up the corners of his lips. He glanced at James, "You running logistics?"

"Happy to," James said. "I've been told begging and tape are the cornerstones of civilization."

"Accurate," Dennis said. "And tetanus boosters. But that's a separate line item. Let's get this party started." So, they moved. It was the only way to keep Claire's nerves from staging a coup. Walt supervised, tail thumping, as they went to work.

"Okay," she said after an hour of controlled whirlwinds. "We've got the revised layout, a second waste station if I can sweet-talk the hardware store into a donation, and at least two new sponsors thanks to James's mysterious connections." She glanced at him.

He shrugged, unbothered. "Just cashed in on a couple of favors is all."

"Semantics," she murmured, but the smile escaped anyway.

Dennis watched the exchange with a professional's eye and a friend's patience. He caught Claire's gaze across the room and gave her a look she recognized from the park— the one that said *I see you, and it's okay.* She returned it with a small smile, and that was enough. Some conversations only need to happen once.

"Alright," Dennis said, clapping his hands together. "You any good at tying balloon arches?" he asked James.

James looked up. "I'll give it my all."

"Great. You just got promoted."

They fell back into work. The room felt lighter, as if a knot had untied in the center of them. When Dennis stepped away to check his messages, James rested a hand on Claire's shoulder. "Everything okay?" he asked quietly, not prying, just offering a place to put the answer if she chose to.

"Yes. He is very kind," she said. It surprised her how true the word felt. "He's in for Saturday. Nail trims and other pet services. He's a good man."

"Good," James said. "The world needs more of all of the above."

Her phone buzzed again. Tina: *Council approved the revised layout. You're good, but they want proof of a second waste station by noon tomorrow.*

She whooped so loud Walt barked. "Approved." She spun the phone toward them. "We're on!"

James broke into a grin. Dennis fist-pumped. She added *WASTE BIN #2* to the list and drew a box so satisfying it felt illegal.

The sun slid lower, turning the front windows into warm squares. Customers came and went: a teenager with a bag of jerseys, a couple with two dogs who had chased a squirrel through a mud puddle, an older woman who always brought her crossword, a man who asked if he could use the change machine even though he didn't need change, only conversation.

When Dennis packed up to make an evening house call, he paused at the door. "Hey, Claire?"

"Yeah?"

He tipped his chin toward the sign. "In case the weather turns, I've got two pop-up tents in my garage. I'll drop them by tomorrow."

"Thank you."

"Don't thank me yet," he said, deadpan. "Wait until I forget the stakes and one of them takes flight and causes collateral damage. You have insurance, right?"

"Noted—and yes," she said, laughing.

He flicked a glance toward James, gave him a small nod that felt like an exchange of unspoken instructions—*Don't hurt her.* Then he was gone, the bell chiming once like a period at the end of a paragraph she didn't need to reread to understand.

Claire let herself breathe. James leaned his hip against the counter and watched her with a careful, delighted look, indicating he had found new evidence that she could, in fact, accept help without turning into a statue.

"So," he said. "Second waste station."

"I can get the bin tomorrow," she said. "If the hardware store lady doesn't make me trade my firstborn for it, that is."

"I have a coupon there that might as well be magic," he said. "Friend of the owner."

"Of course you do." She hesitated. "Is there anyone you *aren't* connected to in some way?"

James chuckled. "I work with a lot of businesses. I know a lot of people."

"Well," Claire started, "thank you. For the dress. For the sponsors. For being... here."

He opened his mouth, then seemed to decide against

whatever his first instinct had been. "I like being here," he said instead.

The dryers rotated, soft thuds of things becoming cleaner. Outside, the sky went violet as the day began to draw to a close. Walt sighed in his sleep as Claire picked up her list and drew a tiny heart next to **Layout Approved**, then pretended she hadn't. James noticed and pretended he hadn't noticed noticing.

"Tomorrow," she said, mostly to herself. "I'll go get the bin. And the map printouts. And cupcakes."

"I'll drive," he said.

She looked up. "You don't have to."

"I know." He smiled, slow and a little reckless. "But I want to."

The moment stretched, not empty, just full of things they *could* name if they wanted to risk them, but they didn't. Not yet, anyway. The bell chimed again—Mrs. Hennessey with a wash-and-fold pickup slip, spewing opinions about leash laws. Their moment folded itself neatly and waited its turn.

By closing, the list had more check marks than empty boxes. Claire locked the door and flipped the sign to CLOSED, then stood with her forehead against the glass for a second, watching the streetlights blink on one by one.

"You look like a person who deserves takeout with her feet up," James said.

"I look like a person who might cry if she has to cook anything," she admitted.

"Then let's not tempt fate. No time for tears." He picked up his coat. "Come on. I'll walk you home. We'll eat something with zero nutritional value and pretend it's healthy."

Claire knew she should have said it was too much. She

should have insisted she was fine. Instead, she reached for the light switch. "Okay," she said. "Let's go."

The Logistics of Hope

CLAIRE

Chapter 23

THE PLANNING MEETING WITH TINA WAS
supposed to take an hour. It took three.

They met at the laundromat because Claire couldn't
leave Walt, and because the folding table doubled as a
conference table if you moved the laundry baskets and
pretended the detergent bottles were a centerpiece. Tina
arrived with a binder—an actual, color-coded, tabbed
binder—and a look on her face that Claire recognized as
Professional Optimism masking Professional Panic.

"Before you open that," Claire said, pointing at the binder, "how bad is it?"

Tina opened the binder. "The permit is delayed."

"Delayed how?"

"The parks department lost our application. Not metaphorically. Literally lost it. Jane at the front desk said it might be 'in a pile somewhere' and that she'd 'get to it.' I asked when, and she said, and I quote, 'When I get to it.'"

Claire closed her eyes. "Okay. What else?"

"The balloon vendor canceled. Apparently, there's a helium shortage."

"A *helium* shortage?"

"Global supply chain issue. I googled it. It's real. So unless we want to blow up three hundred balloons by mouth—"

"We don't."

"—we need a Plan B for the arch. Dennis said he'd build one out of regular balloons and a YouTube tutorial, but I want to manage your expectations on that."

"My expectations are already on the floor, Tina. They're subterranean."

Tina turned a page. "The park sprinkler system is on a timer that no one knows how to change. It goes off every morning at eight-thirty. Our setup starts at seven."

"So everyone gets sprinkled?"

"Drenched, more accurately. The system is industrial. It's like standing in a car wash." Tina paused. "I called the parks department about it. Jane said she'd 'look into it.'"

"I'm sensing a theme with Jane."

"Jane *is* the theme." Tina closed the binder and looked at Claire. "Here's the thing. The permit will come through—I'll go down there tomorrow and stand at Jane's desk until she finds it. The balloons, Dennis can handle.

The sprinklers, we work around. None of this is unfixable."

"Then why do you look like you're about to tell me my dog died?"

Tina hesitated. "Because the pet adoption agency called. They can only bring four dogs instead of twelve. Something about staffing and transport costs."

Claire's stomach dropped. The adoption showcase was the heart of *Yappy Hour*—the entire reason she'd started planning it. Twelve dogs from the county shelter, each one needing a home, each one getting a chance to meet potential adopters in a low-pressure, community setting. Four dogs were better than zero, but it wasn't the same.

"How much would it cost to cover the transport for the other eight?" Claire asked, already knowing she couldn't afford the answer.

"About four hundred dollars for the van rental and an additional handler."

Claire did the math. She had exactly enough in her operating account to cover it—if she didn't eat for two weeks and Walt switched to a diet of hope and tap water.

"I can cover it," she said.

"Claire—"

"I said I can cover it. Those dogs need to be there. That's the whole point."

Tina studied her for a moment, then pulled out her phone. "Or... I could call Jet, who I happen to know has a cargo van for his band equipment and is working at the event on Saturday. And I could call Carla, who I happen to know is a sucker for shelter dogs and would absolutely volunteer to be the additional handler. And we could cover the transport for the cost of gas and Carla's ego."

Claire blinked. "You already called them, didn't you?"

"I called them in the car on the way here." Tina grinned. "Jet said, and I quote, 'Of course. What time?' Carla said, and I quote, 'I was born for this. But, tell Claire she owes me wine.'"

Claire pressed her hands against her eyes. She was not going to cry in front of Tina over a cargo van. She was not.

"I also confirmed the coffee sponsorship with Ben," Tina continued, flipping to another tab. "They're donating fifty cups. Gia is handling all the food samples from *Charmed to Table*. The pet supply store on Birch is donating grooming kits for the gift bags. Mrs. Hennessey— who I did not ask—apparently called the church auxiliary, and they're bringing folding chairs and a pop-up tent."

"Mrs. Hennessey volunteered?"

"Mrs. Hennessey *organized*. She has a phone tree. Claire, she has an actual phone tree. I think she's been waiting for someone to give her a purpose since she retired."

Claire laughed—an overwhelmed laugh that was dangerously close to crying. "I don't know what I did to deserve this."

"You built something people want to show up for. That's not nothing." Tina closed the binder with a decisive snap. "Now. Let's talk about the layout. I have a diagram. It's color-coded."

"Of course it is."

They spent the next two hours mapping the park into zones: the adoption area near the fountain, the vendor tables along the walking path, the grooming station under the big oak, the raffle tent near the gazebo, and a dedicated "Dog Photo Booth" that Tina had conceived of at two a.m. and couldn't be talked out of.

"People love photos of their dogs," Tina argued. "It's basically currency."

"Where are we getting a backdrop?"

"I have a bedsheet and a can of spray paint. It'll be fine."

Claire looked at Tina—organized, stubborn, slightly manic, holding a color-coded binder that represented hours of unpaid work done for no reason other than friendship and the belief that this event mattered—and felt something crack open in her chest. Not grief this time. Something warmer.

"Thank you," Claire said. "For all of this. I know it's a lot."

"It's not a lot. It's a community event for dogs. This is literally the least stressful thing in my life right now." Tina paused. "My mother-in-law is visiting next week. *That's* a lot."

Claire grinned. "I'll send wine."

"Send whiskey. And a getaway car." Tina gathered her binder and stood. "Same time Thursday for final walk-through?"

"Thursday works."

After Tina left, Claire sat at the folding table surrounded by diagrams and lists and budgets, and for the first time since she'd started planning *Yappy Hour*, she thought: *This might actually work.*

Walt, as if sensing the shift in her energy, wandered over and placed his chin on the table next to the layout diagram. He sneezed directly onto the Dog Photo Booth zone.

"I'm choosing to interpret that as enthusiasm," Claire told him.

The Pin and the Beginning

JAMES

Chapter 24

IT HAD BECOME A PATTERN. SOMEWHERE BETWEEN the dress disaster and the permit crisis, James had started showing up at closing time—not every night, but enough that Walt had stopped barking when he heard the bell and started trotting to the door with his leash in his mouth instead.

James didn't so much walk Claire home as relocate together vertically. The joke wrote itself: up the narrow stairwell from the laundromat to her apartment, three flights of evidence that convenience could, in fact, be romantic.

They ordered Thai food from the place down the block that Claire swore had the best pad thai within fifty miles, and ate it cross-legged on her living room floor because the kitchen table was covered in Yappy Hour supplies. Walt positioned himself equidistant between them, his head swiveling between their plates like a furry tennis spectator, while Chaos fell asleep inside an empty takeout bag.

"My dog is in a bag," James observed.

"Your dog fits in a bag. That's the difference between our lives."

They talked until the food was cold and the conversation was warm. Not about the event, or the dress, or the dryer, or any of the logistical disasters that had defined the past week. Claire told him about learning to ride a bike in the parking lot behind the laundromat, her dad jogging beside her with one hand on the seat, and how she'd been so angry when she realized he'd let go blocks ago. James told her about building his first computer at fourteen from parts he'd found at a garage sale, and how his mother had called it a waste of time—three months before he sold a program he'd written on it for enough money to buy his first suit for a job interview.

"We both built something from scraps," Claire said, and the observation landed between them with more weight than she'd intended.

"Yeah," James said quietly. "I guess we did."

At some point, the conversation shifted from words to silence to the kind of closeness that didn't require either. They ended up on the couch—Claire's head on his chest, his arm around her shoulders, Walt sprawled across both their laps like a seventy-pound blanket. James pressed his lips to the top of her head.

"I should go," he murmured.

"Probably."

Neither of them moved.

"Or I could stay and help with the morning shift."

"You'd be terrible at it."

"Probably," he agreed.

She tilted her face up. "Stay."

He kissed her softly. "Okay."

Morning arrived, painting a stripe of sun across the hardwood and the sound of a washer downstairs starting its first brave cycle of the day. James made coffee with the reverence of a man who understood and embraced his role in the chaos of Claire's day. She, hair in a knot that had declared independence at dawn, read through her to-do list like it was a sacred—and somewhat terrifying—text.

"Second waste station by noon," she said, tapping the item. "Hardware store dragon to appease. Map printouts. Cupcakes, if bribery is still legal."

"Bribery is another cornerstone of civilization," James said, handing her a mug of steaming coffee. "It's not from *Cold Brew on Main*, but I'm proud of it." He grinned.

"You said begging was the cornerstone yesterday."

"Civilization is complicated. A duplex, even."

She tried not to smile and failed almost immediately. When she did, something in his chest settled, calming his entire nervous system. *Weird... but kind of nice,* he thought.

They took the stairs down together, Walt thundering

ahead. The hardware store was only three blocks away, but James insisted on driving because his coupon—rumored to be enchanted—lived in his glove compartment next to a flashlight and an emergency tie.

As they wandered the aisles of the hardware store, Mrs. Hennessey, the neighborhood gossip (not to mention, grump!) appeared, intercepting them in aisle five, near the trash bins. The look on her face stole the optimism right from their steps. "Afternoon," she said, her eyes sliding to the way their shoulders aligned, then narrowing. "I do hope your event tomorrow will not encourage further off-leash anarchy."

"Mrs. Hennessey," Claire said, summoning her best customer-service smile. "So nice to see you. We're adding a second waste station. And signage. It should be a smooth-running event. No worries!"

James added, "We also secured a donation of compostable bags and an on-site mobile vet." He folded his arms across his chest, trying his work-confident look on for size with Mrs. Hennessey.

She glanced from James to Claire and back, then adjusted her glasses on the bridge of her nose. "Well. That is... unexpectedly competent."

"Thank you," Claire said, as if it were a compliment. Maybe today—from her—it was. Mrs. Hennessey nodded in their direction with an upturned nose and, with a final scowl, turned on her heel and walked in the opposite direction, right out the door.

"Did she even buy anything?" asked Claire.

"Doesn't appear that way. I guess she was just in here for the free entertainment," James said, grinning and poking Claire in the ribs.

"I don't really think we're all that entertaining, wandering the aisles searching for garbage bins..."

James smirked. "Would have been last night, though."

"Shush," Claire said, her lips upturning slightly as she changed the subject. "Look, the bins!"

James nodded as he reached out to grab one of the industrial-sized garbage containers and wheeled it toward the checkout area. Claire sped up to get in front, moving rogue inventory as they made their way down the aisles.

At the register, the owner eyed the industrial bin. "This one's certainly sturdy," she said. "You'll need two bungee cords with this," she decided, assessing the bin and stack of laminated arrows James snuck onto the counter. She glanced at James, then at Claire, before grinning. "You still owe my sister a pie."

"News sure travels in this town. It's cooling as we speak," he vowed solemnly.

"This is on the house. See you at the event," the owner said, grinning.

Outside, they loaded the bin into the back of James's car and stood there for a second in the crisp light, hands hanging at their sides, fingers not touching but thinking about it.

"Thank you," she said. "For... this. All of it."

He wanted to say, "Of course." He wanted to say, "I like the part where your eyes go soft when you're accepting my help." Instead, he went with: "Anytime."

James dropped Claire off at the print shop while he ran an errand. Then, they made their final stop before returning to the laundromat: the bakery. The cupcakes were frosted to look like tiny dogs of varying sizes and breeds, surrounded by little soap bubbles. To Claire's delight, one of the cupcake models looked exactly like Walter, another, just like Chaos.

James couldn't help but smile at the way Claire squealed and bounced on her toes in excitement as she took in the tiny, perfect images. What she hadn't known was that he'd texted photographs of both dogs to the baker—whose website he had designed back when he was still doing free-lance web design work—during their chaotic event planning endeavors the day before.

She didn't need to know that, though. The joy that spread across her face at the *coincidence* was all the thanks he could ever need.

Back at the laundromat, they staged everything in preparation for the event the next morning: maps were rolled and rubber-banded, signs labeled, treat bags sorted into a pup-pleasing flavor spectrum from chicken to salmon.

As dusk took the edges off the day, James carried the bin down to the park and bolted it to the post where Tina had chalked an X. Claire held the flashlight, two dogs on their leashes, and offered valuable commentary on the process.

"You're very good at pretending this requires two people," she said. "And two dogs."

"It requires one person and a captivated audience," he said. "And, for the record... I prefer my audiences to laugh in the right places."

She laughed in the right place. When he finished securing the bin, she set the flashlight on the bench beside them. The park murmured around them—sprinklers, traffic, a dog arguing with a squirrel it would never catch.

"Do you ever miss not being good at things?" she asked suddenly.

"All the time," he said. "It was simpler being mediocre or at least hiding among the crowd. No one expects the mediocre guy to have all the answers, or any of them for that matter. It got harder when I went off on my own. Nowhere to hide now." He reached for the flashlight. His hand brushed hers and stayed. "Sometimes answers aren't what people need, anyway."

"What do they need?" she asked, her voice quiet.

He paused for a moment, looking at her like the question had an obvious answer. "Maybe just someone else to be there. Someone to listen. Maybe someone to... someone to stay," he said, glancing down, his fingers fidgeting as he realized the vulnerability that had just snuck out. *Why does she make me act like this?!*

Chaos barked at a passing jogger, causing Walt to pull on his leash, almost knocking Claire off her feet. Instead, she stumbled directly into James' arms. For a moment, it appeared as if Chaos and Walt shared a knowing glance. She raised her head to look into James' eyes. The vulnerability spell cracked and reassembled into something less fragile, but maybe a little less *real*.

"Tomorrow's going to be okay," Claire said, straightening and stepping back to put at least a little space between them. "I can feel it."

In the tone of her voice, James could sense a certainty taking over the place in her mind where doubt usually lived. "Of course it is," he said, "and if it tries not to be, we'll make it okay. Better than okay."

Claire nodded and smiled. "Ready to head back?" she asked. James nodded, taking her hand and leading her toward the car.

They drove back, carried in the last of the signs, and climbed the stairs—romance by way of proximity.

The Dryer

CLAIRE

Chapter 25

Two days later, the universe reminded Claire that it didn't care about her love life.

The sound was unmistakable—a grinding, metallic shriek followed by a heavy *thunk* that made the floor vibrate beneath Claire's feet. She froze mid-fold, a pair of someone's khakis suspended in the air.

"No," she whispered. "No, no, no, no, no."

She dropped the pants and rushed to the back of the laundromat, where Machine 3—the largest capacity dryer, the one she'd patched together with duct tape and YouTube tutorials more times than she could count—had stopped spinning entirely. A faint burning smell drifted from the back of the unit.

Claire pressed her forehead against the warm metal and closed her eyes. Machine 3 wasn't just a dryer. It was *the* dryer—the one that handled the king-sized comforters, the bulk wash-and-fold orders, the oversized dog beds she washed for her *Bubbles & Barks* customers. Without it, she'd lose at least thirty percent of her weekly wash-and-fold revenue, which was already barely enough to cover her overhead.

She crouched behind the machine, pulling it away from the wall to access the back panel. The belt was shredded—that much she could see. But the grinding sound suggested something worse. A bearing, maybe. Or the motor itself. She'd replaced the belt twice before on her own, but a motor was beyond her skill set and her tool kit.

She pulled out her phone and called Hank, the only appliance repairman in town who worked on commercial equipment.

"Hank's Repair, this is Hank."

"Hank, it's Claire. Machine 3 is dead again. I think it might be the motor this time."

A pause. "Claire, I was just out there three weeks ago for the belt. If it's the motor, you're looking at a different ballgame. Parts alone are going to run you eight, maybe nine hundred. Labor on top of that. And if the drum bearing went too..." He trailed off diplomatically.

"How much for the whole thing? Worst case?"

"Worst case? Fourteen, fifteen hundred. Could be more depending on what I find when I open her up. Best case, it's just the belt again and a seized bearing—maybe six to eight hundred."

Claire's stomach dropped. She had exactly four hundred and twelve dollars in her business account after last week's supply order. The dog park donation jar had another three hundred, but that wasn't hers to touch.

"Can you come take a look? I need to know what I'm dealing with before I can figure out... anything."

"I can be there Thursday."

"Thursday? Hank, that's four days. I need this dryer."

"I know, sweetheart, but I'm backed up. Mrs. Hennessey's dishwasher exploded—and I mean *exploded*—and I've got two restaurant jobs ahead of you. Thursday's the earliest I can swing it. I'm sorry."

Claire thanked him, hung up, and stood in the back of the laundromat staring at the dead machine as if she could will it back to life. She couldn't. She pressed the heels of her hands against her eyes and took several slow breaths.

This is fine. I've dealt with worse. I'll redirect the big loads to the two medium dryers. It'll take twice as long, but I can manage. I always manage. The thought should have been comforting. Instead, it felt like the lie she'd been telling herself for three years—ever since the last of her parents' savings ran out, and she'd been operating on fumes, stubbornness, and an unhealthy relationship with instant ramen.

James arrived an hour later with Chaos, who sprinted toward the office the moment the leash allowed it. Walt's excited bark echoed through the laundromat.

"Hey," James said, setting a bag of dog treats on the counter—his new habit, since Chaos and Walt's playdates had become a near-daily occurrence. He took one look at Claire's face, and his grin faded. "What's wrong?"

"Machine 3 died."

"The big dryer? Again?"

"This time it might be terminal." She tried to keep her voice light, but it cracked at the edges. "The motor, probably. Maybe the bearings, too. Hank can't get here until Thursday, and the repair could be anywhere from six hundred to fifteen hundred dollars." She paused. "Which I don't have."

James was quiet for a moment. Then: "Let me cover it."

There it was. The offer she'd been dreading from the moment he walked in. Not because it wasn't generous—it was. Not because she didn't need it—she desperately did. But because accepting money from James felt like confirming every fear she had about the gap between them. He could solve her biggest problem with a credit card swipe that wouldn't even register on his monthly statement. For her, it was the difference between keeping her business alive and... she didn't want to think about the alternative.

"No," she said.

"Claire—"

"No, James. Thank you, but no."

He leaned against the counter, studying her. "Can I ask why?"

"Because this is my business. My parents' business. I've kept it going for three years by myself, and I can't start depending on someone else's money to hold it together. Especially someone I've known for..." She counted in her head. "A week and a half."

"It's not about how long we've known each other. It's about someone you care about needing help and you refusing to let them give it."

"It's about not becoming someone who needs to be rescued, James. There's a difference."

The words came out sharper than she intended, and she watched them land. James straightened, his jaw tightening almost imperceptibly. For a moment, the space between them felt wider than the laundromat.

"Needing help isn't the same as needing to be rescued," he said quietly.

"Maybe not. But from where I'm standing, the line between the two is pretty thin."

He was quiet for a long moment. "Okay," he said finally. "I hear you. But if you change your mind—"

"I won't." She softened her voice, aware that she was pushing away kindness because it frightened her. "But thank you. Really. I'll figure it out. I always do."

James nodded slowly. Something moved behind his eyes —not hurt, exactly, but recognition. As if he understood, for the first time, that fixing things for Claire wasn't the same as being there for her, and that the distinction mattered more than he'd realized.

"What if," he said carefully, "instead of paying for the repair, I help you figure out how to pay for it yourself? No money from me. Just... problem-solving. That's what I do."

Claire eyed him suspiciously. "What do you mean?"

"I mean, you have a community event coming up that's generating buzz. You have a dog wash that's underpriced. I looked at your competitors, by the way, and you're charging about forty percent less than anyone within thirty miles. You have a wash-and-fold service with loyal customers who would probably pay a small premium for rush delivery or pickup service if you offered it. And you have a website that looks like it was built in 2006."

"It was built in 2008, thank you very much."

"My point stands." He pulled out his phone. "Give me an hour. I want to show you something."

Claire wavered. This wasn't him writing a check. This was him offering his actual skills, the thing he was good at, the way she'd offered her stain-removal expertise to him. It felt different. Reciprocal, almost.

"One hour," she conceded. "And if your idea involves me selling the laundromat or putting Walt in a commercial, the answer is no."

"Walt would be terrible in a commercial. He'd eat the camera."

"He absolutely would." Claire managed a small laugh. It felt like loosening a valve.

James settled into the office with his laptop while Claire redirected the day's large loads into the smaller dryers, working twice as hard to keep up. She could hear him typing, occasionally muttering to himself or asking Chaos for his opinion on something. By the time the hour was up, he called her over.

"Okay," he said, turning his laptop to face her. "Quick pricing analysis. If you raise the dog wash by five dollars per session—which still keeps you below the competition—and add a premium rush wash-and-fold service at a fifteen percent markup, you'd generate enough additional monthly revenue to cover the dryer repair within six weeks. I can also build you a basic online booking system this weekend that'll make the dog wash side way more efficient. No more phone tag."

Claire stared at the screen. The numbers were clean, simple, and made irritating sense. "You did all of this in an hour?"

"Fifty-three minutes. Chaos needed a potty break."

She wanted to be annoyed that he'd just casually optimized her business model in under an hour when she'd been scraping by for years. Instead, she felt something she hadn't expected: relief that wasn't tinged with shame.

"This is... actually really helpful," she admitted.

"I know." He grinned. "And it didn't cost you a dime. Just your pride, slightly."

"My pride is very expensive."

"I've noticed." He closed the laptop. "So, what do you think?"

Claire looked at the numbers one more time, then at James, then at Machine 3 sitting silent and useless in the back. "I think you might be annoyingly good at this."

"I prefer 'impressively good,' but I'll take annoying."

She shook her head, but she was smiling. And when she reached for a pen to jot down the pricing changes, her hand brushed his on the desk. Neither of them moved it.

"Thank you," she said. "For not just throwing money at it."

"Thank you for not letting me," he replied. "I needed someone to tell me that's not always the answer. I'm a slow learner, but I get there eventually."

"I've noticed," she said, echoing his words back at him. "Now get out of my office. I have laundry to fold, and you're taking up Walter's napping space."

The Discovery

CLAIRE

Chapter 26

FOR THE FIRST TIME IN YEARS, CLAIRE CAUGHT herself humming while she worked. Not just any song—one of the oldies her mother used to play on the laundromat speakers, the kind that filled the space between the machines with something that felt like home. She was folding a stack of towels with practiced efficiency, Walt dozing at her feet, when the bell on the front door rang, and Bridget Hurley walked in.

Claire hadn't seen her in weeks, which wasn't unusual. Bridget was one of those customers who dropped things off, disappeared, then reappeared when it was convenient. Claire had always assumed she was busy—executive assistants to tech CEOs probably had schedules that didn't leave much room for laundromat chitchat.

"Bridget! Hey," Claire greeted her, hoping the guilt over the original dress didn't show on her face. James had assured her it was handled—that Bridget had taken the replacement without issue—but standing face-to-face with the woman whose three-thousand-dollar garment she'd ruined was a different kind of test.

"Claire, hi," Bridget said with a smile that was friendly enough but carried the polished efficiency of someone who was always en route to her next obligation. "I'm just popping in to grab a few things I dropped off last week. Also, I wanted to say thank you for coordinating with James on the dress thing. He was very gallant about the whole situation. Insisted on the replacement. I told him it wasn't necessary, but he's not exactly the type of man you argue with successfully." She laughed lightly.

"He really isn't," Claire agreed, relaxing slightly.

"Don't. Honestly, accidents happen, and the new one is even nicer. Although," Bridget leaned against the counter conspiratorially, "between you and me, I think he was just trying to rack up brownie points before his big move. You know how it is—new city, new job, wanting everyone to remember you fondly on the way out."

The words landed in Claire's chest like ice water.

"His... move?" Claire repeated, keeping her voice steady through sheer force of will.

Bridget blinked, then her expression shifted—the smallest crack in her composure as she realized she'd said something she shouldn't have. "Oh. I assumed you—I mean, he mentioned you two had been spending time together, so I thought—" She straightened, recalibrating. "I'm sorry. I may have spoken out of turn."

"No, it's fine." Claire forced a smile that felt like holding a cracked plate together with both hands. "I just— he mentioned something about a work opportunity, but I didn't realize it was... definite. Where is it again?"

"Santa Clara. California." Bridget studied Claire's face with what might have been sympathy or might have been professional damage assessment. "VP of Infrastructure for *T.M. Enterprises*. It's a huge deal—Mr. Marzini recruited him personally. The housing is already set up. We've been coordinating his orientation for weeks." She paused. "He hasn't told you any of this?"

"He's mentioned work things," Claire said vaguely. "You know how it is. We've been busy with the event." She gestured around the laundromat as if *Yappy Hour* logistics could explain why the man she'd been sleeping with had failed to mention he was moving three thousand miles away.

Bridget nodded slowly. "Well. I'm sure he's planning to discuss it. The timeline has been intense—Mr. Marzini doesn't exactly operate at a relaxed pace." She reached for the bag of clothes Claire had set on the counter. "Anyway. Thank you for these. And good luck with the event. I heard about it through the office. A few of us may stop by."

"That would be great," Claire heard herself say. "Thanks, Bridget."

After the door closed behind her, Claire stood very still. Walt, sensing the shift in energy, lifted his head from his bed and let out a low whine. She didn't look at him. She couldn't look at anything. Her eyes were fixed on the counter where Bridget's bag had been, but she wasn't seeing it.

VP of Infrastructure. Santa Clara. Housing already set up. Orientation for weeks.

Weeks.

He'd known for weeks. Before the laundry lessons. Before the dinner. Before the dress and the bleach and the bed and the way he'd held her and said, "I've never once wanted to run from you."

Weeks.

Claire's hands were shaking. She pressed them flat against the counter and breathed—in through her nose, out through her mouth—the way she did when a customer's irreplaceable heirloom came out of the wash wrong, and she had to figure out a fix before the panic consumed her.

But this wasn't a stain. This wasn't fixable with cold water, vinegar, and a steady hand. This was a man who had walked into her life, dismantled every wall she'd spent years building, and neglected to mention that he had an expiration date.

She picked up her phone and stared at his name. *James Shirt.* She'd never even changed the contact name. She'd been afraid that giving him a real name in her phone would make it real, and real things could be lost.

Turns out he was already lost. I just didn't know it yet.

She didn't text him. She didn't call. Instead, she put the phone face down on the counter, walked into the office, sat on the floor next to Walter, and buried her face in his fur.

Walt, for once, was perfectly still. He didn't squirm or try to lick her face or bat at her with his paw. He just sat there, solid and warm and present, the way he always was when things fell apart. He'd done this when the pipes burst last winter. He'd done this the night she found her father's reading glasses in the back of a drawer and cried for an hour.

He couldn't fix anything, but he could be there, and sometimes that was enough.

It wasn't enough right now. But it was something.

Claire pulled back and looked at Walt's face. He had a button—one of her mother's, a small brass one—stuck in the fur near his ear. She didn't know how it had gotten there. She plucked it free and held it in her palm, this tiny piece of a life that no longer existed, connected to a jar that James had helped her refill on his hands and knees, crawling across this same floor, handling each button like it mattered.

He made me believe he was staying. Not with words— with everything else. With showing up. With buttons and laundry lessons and dog treats and a five-hundred-dollar advance on a service I would have given him for free. He built himself into my life like he was planning to live in it.

She closed her fist around the button. The edges bit into her palm.

A customer rang the bell out front, and Claire stood, wiped her eyes with the back of her hand, and smoothed her shirt. She took a breath, then another, then walked out of the office with the particular steadiness of a woman who had learned, years ago, that the world doesn't stop turning just because yours has.

"Hi," she said to the customer. "How can I help you?"

Her voice didn't crack. She considered that a victory.

The Unraveling

JAMES

Chapter 27

JAMES KNEW SOMETHING WAS WRONG WHEN Claire didn't text him back. Not for an hour, which was normal. Not for three hours, which was unusual. But for an entire day—radio silence. No sarcastic comebacks. No dog photos. No updates about *Yappy Hour*. Nothing.

He told himself she was busy. The event was in two days, and she'd been running on fumes and coffee for a week. He told himself a lot of things while he paced his kitchen, Chaos watching him from his bed with the patient, concerned expression of a therapist who was also a puppy.

"She's fine," he told Chaos. "She's just busy." Chaos tilted his head. "Don't look at me like that."

By the following morning—one day before *Yappy Hour* —the silence had become a wall he couldn't see over or around. He drove to the laundromat.

The bell rang when he walked in. Claire was behind the counter, sorting a pile of receipts with the focused intensity of someone performing surgery. She didn't look up.

"Hey," he said. "I've been texting. Everything okay?"

"Busy." The word came out flat. Surgical.

"Claire."

She looked up, and the expression on her face hit him like a fist. It wasn't anger—not yet. It was worse. It was the careful, measured look of a woman who had been given time to think and had used every second of it.

"When were you going to tell me about California?" she asked.

The floor dropped out from under him. He stood there, mouth slightly open, watching every carefully constructed scaffolding of avoidance collapse in real time. "How did you—"

"Bridget." Claire's voice was steady, but her hands weren't. She pressed them against the counter. "She came in to pick up her clothes. She assumed I knew. Because why wouldn't the woman you've been sleeping with know that you're moving to the other side of the country?"

"Claire, I was going to—"

"When? After *Yappy Hour*? After you helped me set up the event, played with my dog, and kissed me in front of the whole town? When exactly was the plan, James? Because from where I'm standing, it looks like there wasn't one."

He stepped closer. She stepped back.

"It's not that simple," he started, and even as the words left his mouth, he knew they were the wrong ones. They were the words of a man who'd spent his whole life solving other people's problems and avoiding his own.

"It is exactly that simple," Claire said. "You had information. Important information. Information that directly affected me—affected *us*—and you chose not to share it. You didn't forget. You didn't run out of time. You *chose* not to tell me."

"Because I didn't want it to be real!" The words burst out louder than he intended. Chaos, asleep in the office, startled awake and let out a bark. Walt's head appeared over the half-door, ears alert. "I didn't want to tell you because telling you would make it real, and if it was real, then I had to deal with it, and I don't—I can't—" He ran both hands through his hair. "I've been dodging their calls for days. I haven't signed the housing forms. I haven't confirmed the flight. I've been standing in the middle of my own life refusing to move in either direction because both options feel like losing something."

Claire stared at him. A washing machine behind them clicked into its spin cycle, the hum filling the silence like a third voice in the room.

"Both options," she repeated. "So I'm an *option* now? I'm one side of a pros-and-cons list you've been running in your head while you smiled at me and held my hand and told me you'd never wanted to run from me?"

"That's not what I—"

"Because I didn't sign up to be someone's 'maybe.' I've been someone's 'maybe' before. My parents spent their entire lives being *definite* about each other, about this place, about me. And when they died, I promised myself that if I ever let someone in, it would be someone who was sure. Not someone weighing me against a corner office."

"I'm not weighing you against—"

"A VP title, a mansion in California, a salary that probably has more zeroes than my annual revenue? You're not weighing me against that?" She let out a sound that wasn't quite a laugh. "James, I can't even afford to fix my dryer. I live above a laundromat. My entire net worth is probably less than your car payment. I was never going to win that math."

"It was never about the math, Claire."

"Then what was it about?"

He was quiet for a long moment. "It was about being afraid that if I chose, I'd choose wrong. My whole life, my parents chose wrong—chose the job over each other, chose the move over stability, chose ambition over being present. And I told myself I'd never be like them. But then I got this offer, and I realized I'm exactly like them. Because my first instinct wasn't to turn it down. My first instinct was to figure out how to have everything without giving anything up."

Claire stared at him. The anger was there now, but underneath it was something rawer. "You want to know what's funny? Not funny ha-ha. Funny in the way that makes you want to scream into a pile of laundry."

He waited.

"My parents died within eight months of each other. My mom first, then my dad. I think he just... gave up. And after they were gone, I stood in this laundromat—*their* laundromat—and I made myself a promise. I promised that I would never let someone become so essential to my life that losing them could break me the way losing my mom broke my dad." She swallowed hard. "And then you walked in with a coffee stain on your shirt and a puppy named Chaos, and in the span of a week, you made me forget every single wall I'd built. Every. Single. One."

"Claire—"

"I'm not finished." Her voice cracked, but she held it together. "Do you know what it feels like to find out from someone else—from *Bridget Hurley*—that the person you're falling for has a plane ticket and a mansion waiting for him in California? Do you know what that does to someone who has already lost everyone? It doesn't feel like logistics, James. It feels like being left. Again."

The silence that followed was deafening. Even the machines had gone quiet between cycles, as if the laundromat itself was holding its breath.

James opened his mouth. Closed it. Opened it again. "You're right," he said quietly. "About all of it. I should have told you. I should have told you the first night, at dinner, when my phone kept going off, and you asked about it, and I said it was nothing. It wasn't nothing. It was Bridget asking about my housing preference. And I sat there across from you, listening to you talk about your parents, watching you laugh until you cried over my stupid microphone story, and I thought—if I tell her now, this ends. This perfect, impossible thing that I don't deserve and definitely didn't plan for—it just ends."

"So you let me fall without a net."

"I let us both fall without a net. I'm not standing on solid ground here, either, Claire."

She shook her head slowly. "That's the difference between us, James. You *chose* not to have a net. I didn't have one to begin with."

He reached for her hand. She pulled it back.

"I think you should go," she said. "I have an event to

finish setting up. I've been doing this alone for a long time. I can keep doing it alone."

"You don't have to—"

"I know I don't *have* to. But right now, I need to. Please." Her eyes were bright with tears she was refusing to let fall, and it was the refusal that gutted him more than the tears ever could. "Just go."

James stood there for a long moment. He wanted to fix it. Every instinct in his body screamed at him to say the right thing, pull out his wallet, call in a favor, find the solution. But this wasn't a stained dress. This wasn't a broken dryer. This was a woman asking him to leave, and the only right thing to do—the only thing that didn't make him exactly the kind of person she was afraid he was—was to listen.

"Okay," he said. "I'll go." He walked to the office door and crouched to pet Walt, who licked his hand. Then he scooped up a sleeping Chaos and held him against his chest. At the front door, he turned back.

"For what it's worth," he said, "I'm sorry. Not for wanting to stay. For not telling you I was supposed to leave."

The bell chimed as the door closed behind him. Claire waited until his car pulled away from the curb before she let herself cry.

Wine and War Council

CLAIRE

Chapter 28

CLAIRE DIDN'T CALL CARLA. SHE DIDN'T HAVE TO. Carla had a sixth sense for emotional catastrophe—a gift she attributed to "growing up Italian" and Claire attributed to Carla being constitutionally incapable of minding her own business, in the most loving way possible.

She showed up forty-five minutes after James left, carrying a bottle of red wine, a bag of salt and vinegar chips, and an expression that suggested she was prepared to commit felonies if required.

"I saw his car leave," Carla said, pushing past Claire and

heading straight for the kitchen. "His face looked like a crumpled receipt. Your face looks worse. Sit down."

"How did you even—"

"My favorite remote work café overlooks the parking lot, Claire. I see everything. I'm basically a surveillance state with better hair." She pulled two glasses from the cabinet— she knew where they were, having put them there herself during one of her "reorganizing Claire's life" phases—and poured generous amounts of wine into both.

Claire sat on the living room floor because the couch felt too far away and the floor felt more honest. Walt immediately positioned himself beside her, resting his head on her thigh with the gravitational certainty of a dog who understood his job. Carla sat cross-legged across from her, handed her a glass, and waited.

"He's moving to California," Claire said.

"I know. You mentioned."

"He's known for weeks."

Carla's eyes narrowed. "Weeks."

"Before the laundry lessons. Before dinner. Before..." She gestured vaguely at the bedroom.

"Before the sex?"

"Before the sex."

Carla took a very long sip of wine. "I'm going to need you to walk me through the exact timeline, because I want to make sure my rage is correctly calibrated before I decide between a strongly worded text message or arson."

Despite everything, Claire almost smiled. "Please don't commit arson on my behalf."

"I make no promises." But Carla's voice softened. "Tell me everything."

So Claire did. She told her about Bridget coming in, the casual mention of the move, the housing that was already arranged. She told her about the fight—every word she'd said and every word he'd said and the silence in between. She told her about the phone buzzing at dinner, the dodge, the way he'd looked at her over the table like she was the only person in the room while keeping an entire relocation plan in his back pocket.

When she finished, Carla was quiet for a long time. This was unusual. Carla was quiet the way earthquakes were quiet—briefly, and usually right before something significant happened.

"Do you love him?" Carla asked.

The question landed like a dropped plate. Claire stared at her.

"Don't look at me like I asked you to solve calculus. It's a yes-or-no question. Do you love him?"

"I've known him for two weeks."

"That's not what I asked."

Claire looked down at Walt, who looked up at her with the infinite patience of a dog who had all the time in the world and no opinions about human relationships.

"Yes," she whispered. "Which is so, *so* stupid."

"It's not stupid."

"It's pretty stupid. I fell in love with a man who's leaving. That's literally the plot of every sad movie I've ever mocked."

"First of all, those movies are good, and you've always secretly loved them. Second—" Carla set her wine glass down. "He didn't leave. He didn't *tell* you he was leaving. There's a difference. One is a decision. The other is cowardice."

"Or fear."

"Same thing, when it hurts someone."

Claire took a drink of wine. It was cheap and too sweet

and exactly right. "The worst part isn't that he might leave. The worst part is that I let myself believe he wouldn't. I saw all the signs—the job, the phone calls, the way he talked about his career like it was the only thing that mattered—and I rewrote them into something prettier because I wanted him to stay. I did this to myself."

"No," Carla said firmly. "You opened yourself up. He's the one who wasn't honest about what he was walking into. You don't get to blame yourself for trusting someone who gave you every reason to trust them." She reached across the space between them and squeezed Claire's hand. "Your parents would say the same thing."

Claire's eyes burned. "My parents would say I should have checked his LinkedIn before the first date."

Carla laughed—a short, surprised bark of a laugh that startled Walt. "Your dad absolutely would have. Your mom would have invited him over, read his energy, and known within five minutes if he was worth your time."

"What do you think she'd say?"

Carla considered this carefully. "I think she'd say that anyone who gets on his hands and knees to pick up buttons off a laundromat floor is worth giving a second chance. But that second chances have conditions, and the most important one is honesty."

Claire wiped her eyes with the back of her hand. "When did you get wise?"

"I've always been wise. You just never listen because you're too busy folding things." Carla refilled both their glasses. "Now. What are you going to do about *Yappy Hour*?"

"I'm going to do it. Without him."

"Good."

"And I'm going to be amazing at it."

"Obviously."

"And I'm probably going to cry at some point during my speech."

"Also obviously. I'll be in the front row with tissues and a threatening stare for anyone who looks at you wrong." Carla raised her glass. "To doing it scared."

Claire clinked her glass against Carla's. "To doing it scared."

They sat on the floor until the wine was gone and the chips were crumbs, talking about nothing and everything—about Matt's new obsession with sourdough, about Gia's pregnancy scare that turned out to be bad sushi, about the time in seventh grade when Claire tried to bleach her hair and turned it green. They laughed until they cried and cried until they laughed, and somewhere in the middle, the weight on Claire's chest shifted from unbearable to something she could carry.

When Carla left, pressing a kiss to Claire's forehead and whispering, "You're going to be fine. You're always fine. It's annoying, honestly," Claire stood in her apartment and looked at the space where James had been. The dent in the couch cushion. The coffee mug he'd used, still in the drying rack. A single dog treat on the counter that Chaos had left behind.

She picked up the treat, held it for a moment, then placed it in a drawer.

Not in the trash. Not yet. Just... put away. For now.

Yappy Hour

CLAIRE

Chapter 29

THE DAY BEFORE *YAPPY HOUR* BEGAN AT DAWN and didn't stop.

Claire arrived at the park at six-thirty with a car full of signs, a trunk full of supplies, and a dog who immediately tried to chase a squirrel into the fountain. She wrestled Walt back, clipped his leash to a bench, and stood in the center of the empty park trying to remember Tina's color-coded layout diagram, which she'd left on the kitchen table.

"Zone A was the adoption area," she muttered, turning in a slow circle. "Or was Zone A the vendor tables? Why are there zones? Why couldn't she just say 'near the fountain' like a normal person?"

Jet arrived at seven, pulling his cargo van into the parking lot with the careful precision of a man transporting precious cargo. Which he was—eight shelter dogs, each in a crate, each looking out through the wire doors with expressions ranging from hopeful to deeply confused. Carla jumped out of the passenger side, wearing a custom shirt that read "I'M WITH THE DOGS," and immediately began unloading crates with the focused intensity of a woman on a mission.

"Where do these go?" Carla called.

"Zone A!" Claire called back, then added, "Which is near the fountain! I think!"

"You think?"

"I left the diagram at home!"

Carla stared at her. "Claire."

"I know."

"It was color-coded."

"I *know.*"

Jet, wisely, said nothing. He carried crates to the fountain area and began setting up exercise pens while the dogs yipped and whined, and one particularly enthusiastic beagle mix tried to dig through the bottom of his crate.

By nine, the park had transformed. Tina arrived with the binder (and a backup copy of the layout diagram, because she was Tina) and began directing vendors to their assigned spots with the authority of an air traffic controller. Matt appeared with folding tables borrowed from his mother, his church, and what Claire suspected was a neighboring town's VFW hall. Mrs. Hennessey's church auxiliary arrived in a caravan of sensible sedans, unloading folding chairs, a pop-up tent, and a hand-

painted banner that read "YAPPY HOUR — EVERY
DOG HAS ITS DAY" in letters that wobbled
charmingly.

Gia and Ben pulled up in the *Charmed to Table* food
truck, which Ben had painted with paw prints for the occasion. Gia leaned out the service window and shouted,
"Where's my girl?" and Claire jogged over to receive a hug
that smelled like cinnamon and rosemary.

"I made dog-friendly biscuits," Gia said, holding up a
tray. "Peanut butter and pumpkin. They're cute. I put little
paw prints on them with a stamp."

"For the dogs?"

"For the dogs *and* the humans. They're delicious.
Don't judge me."

The balloon arch was Dennis's masterpiece. He'd
watched seven YouTube tutorials—a fact he repeated to
anyone within earshot—and constructed a frame from
PVC pipe that he'd apparently had in his garage "for a
project." The project had never materialized, but the arch
did. It took him two hours, three trips to the car for
supplies, and one near-collapse that prompted a string of
veterinary-grade profanity, but by noon, it stood: a
swooping arc of blue, yellow, and white balloons framing
the entrance to the adoption area.

"It's beautiful," Claire told him.

"It's structurally questionable," Dennis admitted. "If
the wind picks up, we pray."

Claire stood back and looked at everything. The vendor
tables were set. The adoption pens were ready, the dogs
inside them already charming every volunteer who walked
past. The food truck was warming up. The banner was
hung. The photo booth—Tina's bedsheet-and-spray-paint
vision—had turned out surprisingly well, with a backdrop

of painted bones and stars that looked whimsical rather than unhinged.

It wasn't perfect. The sprinkler system had gone off at eight-thirty as predicted, soaking three volunteers and one very offended corgi. A box of raffle tickets had blown into the fountain and had to be fished out and dried on the hood of Jet's van. The PA system crackled ominously every time someone tested the mic.

But it was real. It was happening. And she had done this—not alone, but because of a community that had shown up when she'd asked, the same way they'd shown up when her parents died, the same way they'd shown up every day since, in the small and steady ways that small towns do.

That night, Claire sat on the floor of her apartment with Walt's head in her lap, a checklist in one hand, and a half-eaten pint of ice cream sweating on the floor beside her. The apartment felt too quiet. She'd quickly gotten used to James's presence—the sound of him typing at her desk, the low murmur of him talking to Chaos, the way he hummed off-key when he didn't realize she could hear him.

She picked up her phone three times. Put it down three times. The last text in their thread was from two days ago—his: *For what it's worth, I'm sorry.* She hadn't responded. She didn't know how.

Carla had called twice. Dennis had texted once: *Whatever happened, you'll get through it. You always do. Also, the newest balloon arch video I watched is forty-five minutes long. I'm committed to perfection.* Claire had responded with a single heart emoji because words felt like too much.

She looked at the checklist. Every item was checked except one: **Show up.**

"I can do that," she told Walt. He sighed deeply, as if he'd heard this particular pep talk before and was reserving judgment.

She turned off the lights and lay in bed, staring at the ceiling. Sleep came eventually, restless and thin.

The morning of *Yappy Hour* arrived, and for the first time since she'd started planning it, Claire didn't feel jittery with excitement. She felt hollow. Like someone had scooped out the part of her that had been looking forward to this and replaced it with a heavy, dull awareness that the person she most wanted beside her wouldn't be there.

This was always yours, she told herself as she loaded signs into her car at six a.m., Walt watching from the passenger seat with his usual expression of noble bewilderment. *Before James. Before the laundry lessons. Before any of it. This was your idea, your work, your dream. He just... helped carry some of the boxes.*

And the waste station. And the sponsors. And the—

"Shut up," she told her brain, then glanced at Walt. "Not you."

Walt sneezed.

By seven-thirty, she was at the park with Tina, chalking lines and taping arrows to lampposts with fingers that were steadier than her heart. Carla arrived at eight, carrying an industrial-sized coffee thermos and wearing the same "I'M WITH THE DOGS" shirt from the day before.

"You're wearing that again?" Claire asked.

"It's called commitment, Claire. Also, I only own one shirt that fits the theme." She studied Claire's face with the careful attention of a woman who'd spent the previous evening on the floor of this exact person's apartment, drinking bad wine and absorbing the wreckage. "How are you doing? And don't say fine."

"I'm..." Claire kept her eyes on the chalk line she was drawing. "Functional. I'm functional."

"That's actually worse than fine." Carla set the thermos down. "Have you heard from him?"

"No. And I don't expect to."

Carla was quiet for a moment—which, for Carla, constituted extraordinary restraint. Then: "Good. If he shows up, I've prepared remarks."

"Please don't make a scene at my event."

"I would never make a scene. I would make a *statement*. There's a difference." She cracked her knuckles. "Now. Where's the balloon arch stuff?"

Claire almost smiled. Almost.

Dennis arrived at nine with his folding table, his supply bin, and the two pop-up tents he'd promised. He took one look at Claire's face and didn't ask. Instead, he set up his mobile vet station with quiet efficiency, then walked over and stood beside her as she surveyed the grounds.

"You good?" he asked.

"No," she said honestly. "But I will be."

He nodded. "That's the right answer." He handed her a coffee from the *Cold Brew on Main* booth. "Morgan made you a special one—she called it the 'Claire Under Pressure.' It's a triple shot with lavender."

"I'm afraid to ask what a quadruple shot is called."

"The 'Claire Snapped.' She has a whole menu planned out. I talked her out of some of them for your own protection, and possibly hers."

Claire laughed despite herself, and it felt like cracking a window in a stuffy room—not a solution, but a start.

The town arrived. Not all at once, but in the steady, unhurried way small towns assemble—like a quilt being stitched together, one square at a time. Early-bird seniors with folding chairs. Families with strollers and dogs twice the size of their toddlers. Teenagers performing carefully rehearsed indifference while secretly taking photos of every puppy within range.

And dogs. So many dogs. Golden retrievers and chihuahuas and mutts of unknowable origin, dogs in bandanas and dogs in bow ties and one enormous Great Dane wearing a tutu, whose owner shrugged and said, "She picked it out herself."

Claire moved through the crowd, solving small problems as they arose: a vendor whose table collapsed, a raffle ticket mix-up, a child who'd lost her mother and was found being comforted by a very patient golden retriever near the lemonade stand. She solved them all. Not because it was easy, but because this was what she did. She fixed things. She showed up. She kept going.

At one point, she found herself standing near the fountain—the same fountain where she'd tossed coins with her parents as a kid, making wish after wish. She fished a quarter from her pocket and turned it over in her fingers.

I used to wish for them to come back, she thought. *Then I wished for someone who would stay.*

She flipped the coin into the water without making a wish. Some things, she was learning, you couldn't wish for. You had to build them yourself.

Near noon, Claire climbed the gazebo steps. Her stomach did a cartwheel, but she let it. She tapped the mic.

"Hi," she said. The crowd settled. "I'm Claire. Some of you knew my parents. Some of you know me as the laundromat lady, the stain-fighting woman, the one with the crazy dog." A murmur of laughter. Walt, as if on cue, barked once from where Carla held his leash. "And some of you know me as the person who once shrunk an entire football team's jerseys and turned them pink. For that, I'm still making amends."

Real laughter this time. She gripped the mic and continued.

"When I started planning this, I thought it had to be perfect. I thought I needed everything to go right—every vendor, every detail, every person in exactly the right place." She paused. "That's not how life works, is it? Things go wrong. People don't show up the way you expect them to. Plans change. Stains happen." She glanced down at her own shirt and noticed, for the first time, a small smudge of chalk near the hem. *Of course.*

"But here's what I've learned from years of doing laundry—and trust me, I've done a lot of it." She looked out at the crowd, at Dennis calmly trimming a squirming labradoodle's nails, at Carla taking a selfie with Walt and someone's bulldog, at Gia and Ben serving food from their truck with the kind of joy that made everyone around them hungry. "The stains don't ruin the fabric. Sometimes they're just... evidence that you lived in it. That you wore it hard and loved it well."

"This event is about community. It's about the dogs who need homes and the people who need each other. It's about second chances." Her voice wobbled, and she let it. "So, go forth. Pet everything—with permission, of course. Pick up after your dogs. Grab a coffee from Jet and Morgan, who are the best baristas in this town. Eat everything Gia puts in front of you. And please, stop by the *Bubbles & Barks* table on your way out for a free dog wash voucher. Walt and I will be there with bells on." She paused. "Not literal bells. He'd eat them."

Applause. Real, warm, unhurried applause from people who had known her parents and watched her grow up and came today because she'd asked them to—because they *wanted* to. Claire stepped down from the gazebo with tears in her eyes and a smile on her face, and Carla was there with a hug so tight it hurt.

"Your mom would be so proud of you," Carla whispered.

Claire squeezed back. "Don't make me cry. I just did my mascara."

"You're not wearing mascara."

"Exactly. That's how bad things have gotten."

Near two o'clock, Tina jogged up, breathless and grinning. "A council member stopped by. They called the event 'the kind of thing this town needs more of.' Monthly approval, if we want it. And they're fast-tracking the dog park discussion."

Claire stared at her. "Monthly?"

"Monthly. With a budget line."

She pressed both hands over her mouth. Then she whooped, loud enough that Walt barked and three nearby dogs joined in, creating a chain reaction of barking that rippled across the park like a wave.

"We did it," she said. "We actually did it."

"*You* did it," Tina corrected.

Claire shook her head. "No. Look around." She gestured at the park—at the people and the dogs and the volunteers and the small, beautiful chaos of a community showing up for itself. "We all did."

The Return

JAMES

Chapter 30

JAMES SAT IN HIS CAR AT THE EDGE OF THE PARK
for eleven minutes. He knew because Chaos stared at him
for every one of them, and at minute eight, the puppy let
out a whine that roughly translated to, *Are we doing this, or
are we just going to sit here being pathetic?*

"Fair point," James muttered.

He hadn't planned to come. He'd spent the morning
staring at the *T.M. Enterprises* housing packet spread across
his kitchen table, trying to convince himself that this was
what success looked like—glossy photos of California

homes with mountain views and square footage that could swallow Claire's entire laundromat six times over.

The problem was that success had never felt this much like loss.

He'd picked up his phone a dozen times. Typed messages he deleted. *I'm sorry. I miss you. I'm an idiot.* All true, all insufficient. What do you say to someone you hurt not by doing something terrible, but by doing nothing at all? By standing in the middle of their life, letting them build hope around you, while the wrecking ball was already scheduled?

You show up, a voice in his head said. It sounded, annoyingly, like Claire's.

So here he was. Not with a plan. Not with a replacement dress or a favor to call in or money to throw at the problem. Just him and a puppy and the growing realization that the scariest thing he'd ever done wasn't walking into a CEO's office—it was walking across a park toward a woman who had every reason to tell him to leave.

He clipped Chaos's leash to his collar, got out of the car, and walked.

He saw her before she saw him. She was near the gazebo, crouching to help a little girl put a bandana on a squirming beagle mix, laughing at something the kid said. Walt stood beside her like a bodyguard, his tail swishing slowly. She looked tired. She looked happy. She looked like she'd done this without him and survived, and the pride and pain of that realization hit him simultaneously.

Dennis noticed him first. The vet was at his station,

trimming a poodle's nails with practiced ease. He looked up, saw James, and held his gaze for a long, steady beat. James couldn't read the expression—it wasn't hostile, but it wasn't warm. It was the look of a man measuring whether you deserved the second chance you were about to ask for.

James gave a small nod. Dennis returned it, then looked back down at the poodle. Permission granted, conditions pending.

Carla noticed him second. She was less subtle. She elbowed Matt, pointed, then mimed a throat-slitting motion before Matt pulled her arm down and whispered something that made her fold her arms and huff. But she stayed put.

Claire noticed him last. She stood up from the beagle situation, brushed chalk dust off her knees, and turned— and there he was, standing ten feet away with Chaos wriggling in his arms and an expression on his face that she'd never seen before.

He looked scared.

Not the charming, self-deprecating nervousness she'd seen on their first date. Not the avoidant discomfort of a man dodging phone calls. This was real fear—the kind that comes from knowing you might have already lost the thing you're standing in front of.

"Hi," he said.

Claire didn't respond immediately. She looked at him the way she might examine a stain—assessing the damage, determining whether it was treatable or terminal.

"Hi," she said finally.

"I'm not here to fix anything," he said. The words came out rough, unrehearsed. "I know I can't. I know I—I don't have a grand gesture. I didn't bring sponsors or a gift card or a new dress. I just…"

He set Chaos down. The puppy immediately trotted over to Walt, who sniffed him once and lay down, allowing Chaos to curl up against his side. Even the dogs seemed to understand that this moment required quiet.

"I called Tom Marzini this morning," James said. "I told him I wasn't coming to California."

Claire's expression didn't change. "James—"

"Wait. Please. Let me—I need to say this the right way, because I've been saying everything wrong, and you deserve better." He took a breath. "I didn't turn it down for you. I turned it down for me. Because somewhere between the coffee stain and the buttons and the bleach, I realized that I've spent my entire life climbing toward a version of success that my parents wanted for me. Bigger titles. Fancier cities. More money, more status, more proof that I'm enough. And none of it—*none* of it—has ever made me feel the way I felt watching you sort buttons off the floor while two dogs tried to lick my face."

Claire's lip twitched. She was fighting a smile. He took it as permission to keep going.

"I'm going to stay. I'm going to keep consulting, remotely, on my terms. It won't be a VP title. It won't come with a mansion. But it'll be mine. And I want to be here. In this town. In this park. In that laundromat that smells like lavender detergent and dog. I want to be wherever you are —if you'll let me. And if you won't, I still want to be here, because this place is the first place that's ever felt like home, and I should have known that before you had to tell me."

He stopped. The park continued around them—dogs barking, kids laughing, the pop-up tent flapping in the breeze. Claire stood very still.

"You hurt me," she said quietly.

"I know."

"Not by leaving. By not telling me you were going to."

"I know."

"I don't need someone to fix my dryer or buy a waste station or replace a dress, James. I need someone who tells me the truth, even when the truth is hard. Especially when it's hard. Can you do that?"

He didn't hesitate. "Yes."

"Even when you're scared?"

"Especially when I'm scared. I'll probably be bad at it. I've spent thirty-something years perfecting the art of throwing money and charm at my problems instead of talking about them. It's practically a skill at this point."

"A skill you'd like to unlearn?"

"With the help of a very patient laundry teacher, maybe."

Claire looked at him for a long time. Then she looked at Walt and Chaos, curled up together on the grass. Then she looked back at him.

"You can start by helping me take down the balloon arch," she said. "Dennis put it up, but he conveniently has to leave before cleanup."

James exhaled deeply. "I can do that."

"And James?"

"Yeah?"

"The next time you have something to tell me—something big, something scary, something you'd rather avoid—you tell me. At the laundromat, over coffee, during a dog bath, I don't care. You tell me before someone else does. Deal?"

"Deal."

She nodded once, then turned toward the gazebo. After three steps, she stopped and looked over her shoulder.

"Also, you owe me dinner. A real one. You're paying this time. And I'm wearing actual shoes."

He grinned. "Yes, ma'am."

"Don't call me ma'am."

"Yes, Princess."

She rolled her eyes, but she was smiling. And when he fell into step beside her, she let him. Not because it was easy, but because some stains, she was learning, don't ruin the fabric. They just change the pattern. And sometimes— sometimes—the new pattern is better than the original.

Freshly Folded

CLAIRE

Chapter 31

THREE SATURDAYS LATER, THE PARK FILLED again. More people this time, which shouldn't have surprised Claire—word of mouth traveled faster than Walt through an open gate—but it did. She stood at the gazebo railing with a cup of Gia's lemonade and tried to take it all in without letting her chest explode from the sheer fullness of it.

The balloon arch, built by Dennis after an extensive YouTube research phase, looked even better the second time around. ("I watched seven videos this time," he reported proudly. "Three of them were even relevant.") The waste stations stood like sentinels, a tribute to municipal cooperation and James's connections. The adoption board near the entrance held photos of dogs who had found homes after the first event—twelve in total, including the bulldog in the bow tie, who now answered to "Sir Reginald" and lived with Mrs. Hennessey in her immaculate Cape Cod. Mrs. Hennessey, who had been spotted walking him past the laundromat twice a day, pretending the detour was "for her health."

Dennis poured coffee from a thermos into travel mugs and handed one to Claire. "Monthly suits you," he said. "You glow differently. In a way that no longer suggests a medical emergency."

"High praise," she said, rolling her eyes.

"We both know what it is," he said, nodding toward the park entrance as James arrived, Chaos perched like a king atop a crate of donated blankets. He wore a faded T-shirt—not a polo sweater, not a work outfit—and the expression of someone who had already solved three minor problems before nine a.m. and was ready for more.

He kissed Claire. The kind of kiss that tasted like coffee and sleep and the particular comfort of a person who had chosen to stay, not because it was easy, but because easy had never been the point.

"Registration tables need extra pens," he said, already moving. "And Carla is trying to put Walt in a bow tie. I've been asked to intervene."

"By whom?"

"Walt."

Claire watched him jog toward Carla, who was, indeed, chasing Walt with a polka-dot bow tie while Matt filmed. She shook her head and smiled.

Things weren't perfect. James's income had taken a hit after turning down *T.M. Enterprises*, though he'd secured two new consulting clients within the first week—smaller companies, local ones, including the bakery whose website he'd built years ago, and a regional veterinary chain that Dennis had connected him with. He worked from the small desk Claire had squeezed into the corner of the laundromat office, his laptop sharing space with Walter's bed and a jar of lost buttons. Some days, she caught him staring at his phone with a faraway look, and she knew he was doing the math—not on spreadsheets, but on the choices that had led him here instead of there.

She didn't pretend it was simple. She asked him, on those days, if he was okay. Sometimes he said yes. Sometimes he said, "Not yet, but I will be." She was learning that the second answer was the braver one.

He'd started helping with the laundromat in small ways that had become less small over time—upgrading her ancient computer system, building a website that actually worked, setting up an online booking system for the dog wash that tripled her appointments in two weeks. He never asked for credit, and she never let him go without it.

"You're turning my laundromat into a tech startup," she told him one evening, watching him run cable behind the dryers.

"I'm turning your laundromat into a laundromat that exists in the current century," he corrected. "You were still using a paper ledger, Claire. A *paper ledger.* I've seen museums with more modern record-keeping."

"My parents used that ledger."

He stopped, cable in hand, and looked at her. "Then we'll keep it," he said simply. "For the things that matter. The new system handles the rest."

That was the thing about James she was still getting used to—he didn't try to replace what came before. He built around it.

Near noon, Claire took the mic. She kept it short.

"Thank you for showing up," she said. "That's it. That's the whole speech." She paused. "Okay, one more thing. Some stains never come out. But they make the pattern more interesting." She winked at James, who raised his lemonade in a toast from the edge of the crowd. "Now go pet some dogs. Responsibly."

Applause rose and settled. Claire stepped down, and James met her at the bottom with his free hand extended.

"Walk with me?" he asked.

"It's a very long journey to the other side of the gazebo."

"I brought provisions," he said, holding up the lemonade.

They made it four steps before Chaos bolted for the fountain, dragging his leash behind him. Walt, in an uncharacteristic display of speed, lunged after him, pulling Claire forward. James caught her arm, then her waist, then just held on.

"We have to stop meeting like this," she said, laughing against his chest.

"Never," he said. And kissed her.

Around them, the town carried on. Dogs barked. Children shrieked. Mrs. Hennessey was seen smiling at Sir Reginald, though she'd deny it later. The fountain caught the light and threw it back in pieces, the way it always had and always would.

Claire's life wasn't washed, pressed, and folded neatly. But standing there, dog hair on her shirt, lemonade on her shoes, and a man who had chosen to stay holding her close —she thought it was becoming something she loved.

Some messes, she was learning, weren't messes at all.

They were just how the best stories begin.

About the Author

Regina lives in the beautiful Hudson Valley of New York. She holds a B.A. in Environmental Studies and Latin American Studies and a Master's in Public Administration. Before becoming a full-time writer and editor, she worked in fundraising for a global environmental conservation nonprofit and later spent several years at home raising her children.

When she's not writing, you can find Regina gardening, cooking, drinking too much coffee, or spending time exploring the outdoors with her kids and pets.

Other Books

Be sure to check out these other books by Regina:

Poetry: Amidst Fading Blooms; Secrets Unearthed, Petals Unfurled; The Venom and The Rose; Of Weeping & Wildflowers; and Between the Roots and the Roses

Rom-Com:

The Small Town Dirt Series: Dirty Hoe – A Gardening Romance, Dirty Latte – A Coffee Shop Romance;

Pineberry Peak Seasonal Novellas: Faking It on the Slopes of Pineberry Peak – A Holiday Novella, Making It on the Slopes of Pineberry Peak – A Valentine's Day Novella

Middle-Grade Fiction: Paisley, Untethered – A Rescue Dog's Tale

Non-Fiction: But, He Was 6'2": The Red Flags I Missed Because He Was Tall

Get In Touch

Connect with Regina:
Social Media:
Facebook, TikTok, Instagram, Goodreads:
ReginaBergenAuthor
Substack: Regina Bergen Author
Website: www.ReginaBergen.com
Email:
ReginaBergenAuthor@ReginaBergen.com